Have you ever been so busy you had no time for your friends? That happened to me and my best friends, Allie and Darcy. We decided to do something about it. For one whole month, we would spend all our free time together. No extra sports activities, no special projects—and, above all, no dates! Our new motto was "Friends First."

But then things started going wrong. I canceled a sleepover with Allie and Darcy in order to help out an old friend. I volunteered to do extra work for our school newspaper, *The Scribe*, even though I promised Allie and Darcy I wouldn't. And I spent time with a really cute new boy in school, Keir. He asked me out and I really wanted to say yes. But I couldn't!

What could I do? I had to figure out a way to be true to my friends *and* true to myself. Luckily, there were a lot of people I could turn to for advice. There are nine people and a dog in my very full house. There's me, my big sister, D.J., my little sister, Michelle, and my dad, Danny. And that's just the beginning.

When my mom died, Dad needed help. So he asked his old college buddy, Joey Gladstone, and my uncle Jesse to come live with us to help take care of me and my sisters.

Back then, Uncle Jesse didn't know much about taking care of three little girls. He was more into rock 'n' roll. Joey didn't know anything about kids, either—but it sure was funny watching him learn.

Having Uncle Jesse and Joey around was like having three dads instead of one! But then something even better happened—Uncle Jesse fell in love. He married Rebecca Donaldson, Dad's cohost on his TV show, *Wake Up, San Francisco*. Aunt Becky's so nice—she's more like a big sister than an aunt.

Next Uncle Jesse and Aunt Becky had twin boys. Their names are Nicky and Alex, and they are adorable!

I love being a part of a big family. Still, things can get pretty crazy when you live in such a full house!

FULL HOUSE™: Stephanie novels

Available from MINSTREL Books

FULL HOUSE™
Stephanie

Girl Power

Ellen Steiber

A Parachute Book

A MINSTREL® BOOK

Published by POCKET BOOKS

New York   London   Toronto   Sydney   Tokyo   Singapore

This book is a work of fiction. Names, characters, places and incidents are products of the author's imagination or are used fictitiously. Any resemblance to actual events or locales or persons living or dead is entirely coincidental.

A MINSTREL PAPERBACK *Original*

A Minstrel Book published by
POCKET BOOKS, a division of Simon & Schuster Inc.
1230 Avenue of the Americas, New York, NY 10020

A PARACHUTE BOOK

 Copyright © and ™ 1999 by Warner Bros.

FULL HOUSE, characters, names and all related indicia
are trademarks of Warner Bros. © 1999.

ISBN: 0-671-02163-X

First Minstrel Books printing October 1999

10 9 8 7 6 5 4 3 2 1

A MINSTREL BOOK and colophon are registered trademarks of
Simon & Schuster Inc.

Cover photo by Schultz Photography

Printed in the U.S.A.

PHX/✕

CHAPTER
1

◆ ◀ ◆ ◆

Stephanie Tanner hurried through the halls of John Muir Middle School. She had to drop off her makeup history quiz, then get to the other side of the building for biology class. For which she could *not* be late. Mr. Simmons, the new science teacher, gave automatic detentions for coming in after the bell.

How did my life get so hectic? Stephanie asked herself. She missed school two days the week before because she was home with a sore throat. Now she felt as if she had been gone a month.

"Steph, wait for me!"

Stephanie turned. Darcy Powell, one of her best friends, was jogging toward her.

"Hey, Darce, what's up?" Stephanie asked.

"I was going to ask you the same thing," Darcy said with a laugh. Her dark eyes twinkled. "I feel like I haven't seen you forever!"

"I was home sick Thursday and Friday," Stephanie explained.

"Are you okay now?" Darcy asked.

Before Stephanie could reply, Allie Taylor ran over to them. Allie's long, wavy brown hair was pulled back in a scrunchy. "Great, I found you both," she said breathlessly. "So, are you going to do the car wash?"

"What car wash?" Stephanie and Darcy asked together.

"The student council one," Allie began. Her face fell. "Didn't I tell you guys about it?"

"I haven't talked to you since last week," Stephanie said.

"She was out sick," Darcy filled Allie in. "I was out on Friday, too. I flew to Chicago with my parents to see my grandmother. She broke her ankle."

"Really?" Allie sounded shocked. "Why didn't you tell me?"

"Or me!" Stephanie exclaimed. "You know, there's something wrong here. You two are my best friends, and I feel like we've completely lost track of each other."

"Totally," Darcy agreed.

"Why don't you both come over to my house after school today?" Stephanie suggested. "That way we can catch up."

"Can't," Darcy said. "I've got field hockey practice."

"And I've got a student council meeting," Allie chimed in. "How about tomorrow?"

"On Tuesday I've got my *Scribe* meeting," Stephanie said. She was a reporter for their school paper. The bell rang just then, and Stephanie groaned. "Oh, no. Simmons is going to give me a detention. I've got to go."

"Me too," Darcy called. She was already halfway down the hall. "I'll catch you two later."

"If we're really lucky," Allie muttered. She gave Stephanie a helpless look. "See you?"

"Soon," Stephanie promised.

That afternoon—after her science detention—Stephanie walked home from school on her own. She thought about her friends and felt surprisingly lonely. She couldn't remember the last time she'd hung out with Darcy and Allie. She missed them.

Stephanie and Allie had been best friends since kindergarten. When Darcy moved to San Francisco in the sixth grade, Stephanie and Allie knew they'd found another best friend. The three girls did almost everything together.

This year, though, things changed. Darcy was captain of the field hockey team. Allie took piano lessons, plus she was president of the student council. Stephanie was on the staff of the school paper. They barely had time to do their homework, much less hang out together.

Stephanie reached her house and opened the front door. She stepped into the living room and blinked. Living in a house with eight other people meant there was usually someone at home. Today, though, the Tanner household was in overflow mode.

Stephanie's nine-year-old sister, Michelle, and her friend Cassie were playing a board game on the coffee table. Her uncle Jesse's five-year-old twins, Nicky and Alex, and their friends, Michael and Cole, were playing with the twins' train set.

D.J., Stephanie's eighteen-year-old sister, and her friend Kimmy were on their way up the stairs. Even Comet, their dog, had a friend over. Cole's Chihuahua sat beside Comet, watching the miniature train zip around the living room.

"Hi, everyone," Stephanie said.

"Hi, Steph!" Alex called excitedly. "Look, Mommy and Daddy set up the trains for us!"

"Cool," Stephanie said. She stopped to muss

Alex's hair. Then she put her books down and headed into the kitchen. There she found her father and Joey preparing dinner.

Joey was Danny Tanner's best friend. He lived in their house, too. He and Jesse moved in years ago, after Stephanie's mother died. Originally Joey and Jesse were going to help out her dad for just a little while, but they all loved living together. So even when Jesse married Becky and they had twins, they made an apartment for themselves in the attic.

Now Joey emptied a tin of anchovies into a glass mixing bowl. "Are you sure you want me to use these things?" he asked Stephanie's dad. "They look like little dead fish."

"They *are* little dead fish," Danny said. "Trust me. It's going to be delicious."

Stephanie poured herself a glass of milk. "What are you making?" she asked.

Her father set a pot of tomato sauce on the stove. "Pizza," he replied. "Joey is helping me with a topping I dreamed up."

Uh-oh, Stephanie thought. Her father loved to cook. He especially loved to try new—sometimes weird—recipes on his family.

"So, Steph," Danny said, "how's your throat feeling?"

"I'm totally better," Stephanie assured him.

Just a little sad, she thought. *Even my dad gets to spend time with his best friend. And Jesse and Becky are each other's closest friends. So that means I'm the only person—or animal—in this house who isn't hanging out with a best friend!*

Danny stopped kneading dough. He looked at her curiously. "Is something wrong?" he asked.

Stephanie hesitated. There were thirteen people in the house at the moment, plus two dogs. If she said she was lonely, her dad would think she'd lost her mind.

"It's nothing," she said. "I'm going up to my room to finish my *Scribe* article."

"Dinner will be ready in about an hour," Danny said.

Stephanie glanced into Joey's mixing bowl. *Yuck!* she thought, but smiled at her dad and said, "I can't wait."

Stephanie stared at the slice of pizza on her plate. *Would it be really rude to scrape off the anchovies?* she wondered.

She glanced across the table. Both of her sisters had pushed their anchovies to the side of their plates. D.J. caught her eye and grinned. "Great minds think alike," she joked.

Danny raised his hands in defeat. "No anchovies next time."

"Thank you!" Stephanie and her sisters chorused.

Danny's dark eyebrows rose as the doorbell rang. "Who could that be?" he asked, and went to answer the door. Moments later Allie and Darcy trailed him into the kitchen. "Two more victims to try my experimental pizza!" he announced.

"Actually, we just dropped by to see if Stephanie could have dessert with us," Darcy said quickly.

"We're going to the Ice Cream Palace," Allie explained.

"Could I? Please?" Stephanie asked.

"Have three more bites of salad," Danny bargained. "And then you can go."

Stephanie happily finished her salad. Then she cleared her plate from the table, grabbed a jacket, and followed her friends outside. The evening air was cool. She shoved her hands into the pockets of her denim jacket.

"I've really missed you two," Stephanie said. "Do you realize how long it's been since we hung out?"

"Ages," Allie answered. "I mean, I can't believe

I didn't know about Darcy's grandmother. Or your sore throat."

"And neither one of us knew you needed volunteers for the student council car wash," Darcy added.

"We absolutely have to start spending more time together," Stephanie decided.

"That sounds great," Allie said wistfully. "But how? I mean, now that I'm president of the student council, I have to go to a zillion meetings. Plus my piano teacher wants me to be in a recital. Which means I'm supposed to practice nonstop."

Stephanie thought about it. "The problem is, we all have too many activities—and they're all different. We're not even in any of the same classes."

Darcy took a ball from her jacket pocket, tossed it into the air, and caught it. "I have an idea," she said. "There's a swing class starting this week. We could all take it together."

"Swing?" Stephanie asked doubtfully. "Isn't that big band music from the thirties or something?"

"Yeah," Darcy answered. "Haven't you seen that commercial with all those kids in khakis, doing those super-cool swing dance moves?"

"It is hot," Allie admitted. "I was thinking about taking that class, too."

8

"Come on, Steph," Darcy said. "It would be so much fun."

"Okay," Stephanie agreed reluctantly. The moves in that commercial looked awfully complicated to her. "But I still think we need to do more to make sure we spend time together."

Allie pulled open the door to the Ice Cream Palace. "You're right," she said. "Swing class is a start, but it's not enough. We need to make more time for each other."

"We have to put our friendship first," Stephanie agreed. Then she had an idea. "That's it! We'll start our own program. We could call it Friends First."

"And do what?" Darcy wanted to know.

"It's more what we *don't* do," Stephanie explained. "We won't take on new projects that the other two aren't involved in."

"And no dates," Allie added. "At least for a while."

They all ordered and paid for ice cream sundaes. Then they sat down at a table to wait until their order was ready.

"The thing is," Allie went on, "we've really fallen out of touch. We need to take emergency measures."

"She's right," Stephanie agreed. "At this rate,

we'll be lucky if we remember each other's names by the time we graduate."

"It's not *that* bad!" Darcy said.

"Almost," Allie joked. "I say we take the next month to get our friendship back on track. No new projects or dates for one month." She grinned. "And to kick off Friends First—a reunion sleepover at my house this Friday!"

"But I said I'd shoot baskets with Josh on Friday," Darcy protested.

"Tell him you can't," Stephanie insisted. "The whole point of this is that friends have to come first."

Darcy shrugged, then smiled. "Okay," she said. "Friends First?"

Stephanie and Allie cheered. "Friends First!"

CHAPTER
2

◆ ◀ ◆ ◆

Stephanie doodled in the margin of her biology notebook. She knew she should be taking notes. But at least five minutes ago, she lost interest in what Mr. Simmons was saying. Something about cells dividing and mitosis.

My-toes-is . . . she wrote. *My-toes-is* . . . *wiggling*. She drew a sketch of a bare foot with wiggling toes.

"Stephanie Tanner, please see me at the end of class," Mr. Simmons said curtly.

Stephanie gulped hard. She couldn't get another detention today—not when she had her *Scribe* meeting.

Did Mr. Simmons know I was writing silly notes in my margins? she wondered. She scribbed over her doodles just in case.

The end-of-class bell rang. Stephanie walked up to Mr. Simmons's desk. "You wanted to see me?" she asked nervously.

"Yes, I do," he replied. "Do you know why?"

Stephanie decided not to mention her doodling. "No," she said.

Mr. Simmons pointed to her textbook.

"Did I miss a homework assignment when I was out sick last week?" she guessed.

"No, Miss Tanner, you neglected to put a cover on your textbook."

"Oh," Stephanie said. She remembered that Mr. Simmons mentioned covering books on his first day of teaching. "I meant to do it," she explained. "I guess I forgot."

"You forgot? Your textbooks are school property," Mr. Simmons reminded her. "That means the school trusts you to protect them. It's up to you to live up to that trust. So either you cover that book by the time school starts tomorrow, or you can see me after school for another detention. Is that clear?"

"Very," Stephanie said, startled. She couldn't believe he was making such a big deal out of covering a book.

"Fine. I'll expect you to show me your book first thing tomorrow," the teacher told her.

Great! Stephanie thought as she left class. Now she would definitely be late for the *Scribe* meeting. She had to buy a book cover from the school store before it closed.

She rushed down the hall toward the store. A long line of students trailed out from the counter.

Stephanie took her place in line and waited impatiently.

Finally the girl behind the counter said, "Next? We have John Muir T-shirts on sale this week, plus special Raccoon mugs."

"Thanks," Stephanie replied, "but all I need is a book cover."

"Don't tell me," said an amused voice behind her. "You've got Simmons, right?"

Stephanie turned around to see an incredibly cute boy standing behind her. He was about an inch taller than she was. He had straight black hair, blue eyes, and tanned skin.

"Actually," Stephanie joked, "I just have this deep desire to protect school property."

"It's a good thing," the boy replied in a mock-serious voice. "Because the school is trusting you, and you wouldn't want to betray a trust, would you?"

"Never," she said solemnly.

"That will be thirty-five cents," the girl behind the counter said.

"I'll take one of those, too," said the boy. He smiled at Stephanie. "I have Simmons second period," he explained.

"I've got him last," Stephanie said.

The boy gave her a sympathetic look. "What a way to end your day!"

Stephanie laughed. "Tell me about it."

"I'm Keir Cooper," he said. He sounded a little shy.

"Stephanie Tanner," she replied. "How come I haven't seen you around before?"

"My family just moved to San Francisco," he explained, "from Boulder, Colorado. This is my first day at John Muir."

"Well, welcome to John Muir," Stephanie said. "Colorado to San Francisco . . . that must be a huge change."

"I miss the Rockies," Keir admitted. "And all the snow. But it's kind of cool being so close to the Pacific."

"It's great, actually," Stephanie assured him. "In the early fall you can go out on a boat and watch the whales migrate."

Keir paid for his book cover, and they stepped away from the counter. "So," he said.

"So," Stephanie echoed. Suddenly *she* felt shy. She couldn't think of a thing to say. Nervously she examined the inside of her new book cover.

"Step One: Measure the length and width of your textbook's spine," she read aloud. *"Step Two: Fold section A along the dotted line, creating flaps C, D, E, and F. Step Three: Fold over section B, creating flaps G and H . . ."*

Keir grinned. "I've read computer manuals that sounded simpler."

He has a really nice smile, Stephanie decided. *Warm and friendly.* "Do you like computers?" she asked.

Keir rolled his eyes. "I don't have much choice. Both my mom and dad are software engineers. They put me on a keyboard as soon as I could sit up. And my older brother, Jason—he's seventeen—just designed a new computer game. It's a family conspiracy: The Cooper Computer Nerds."

Stephanie didn't think Keir looked anything like a nerd. "So what else do you like besides computers?" she asked.

"Soccer," Keir answered. "In Colorado I played on our team. And I like ice hockey and playing guitar and—oh, no!"

"What?" Stephanie asked.

"My new guitar teacher is showing up at my house"—Keir glanced at his watch—"in exactly *five* minutes. Sorry, but I've got to run."

"Me too," Stephanie groaned. "I totally forgot all about my *Scribe* meeting."

Keir jogged backward down the hall, moving toward the exit. "Maybe I'll see you again?" he called.

"I hope so," Stephanie replied. *The sooner the better!* she thought.

"Stephanie, I'm glad you're here." Ms. Blith, the adviser for the student paper, turned as Stephanie opened the door to the Media Arts room.

"Sorry. I got a little held up," Stephanie apologized.

"No problem," Ms. Blith told her. "I was just saying that we're going to add two pages to each edition of the *Scribe*. Which means we'll need new columns and features. Any ideas?"

"How about a photograph of the month?" Gia, the paper's photographer, suggested. "I don't mean photographs taken by me. Any student in the school could submit a candid shot connected to John Muir."

"That sounds great," said Sue Kramer, the editor of the paper.

"How about a review column for new movies and music CDs?" Bill Klepper suggested.

"Sounds good," Ms. Blith said. "Bill and Sue,

16

why don't you alternate reviews? One of you could do music, the other movies."

"We need a technology column," Quentin Baglio spoke up. Quentin was a seventh grader who never talked about anything but computers. "We could cover Internet sites for middle-school kids."

"I had that same thought, Quentin. And I think you're the perfect person to write it." Ms. Blith started to list the ideas on the chalkboard. "How about a personal opinion column?"

"What do you mean?" Stephanie asked, intrigued.

Ms. Blith turned to face her. "A column in which the writer discusses some personal issue that most kids in the school can relate to."

"Like school spirit?" Tiffany Schroeder asked.

"No, that's about the school," Ms. Blith said. "I want this column to stem from the writer's personal experiences."

Bill groaned. "Like Thanksgiving columns that talk about how grateful we should all be?"

Ms. Blith smiled. "I was hoping for something a little more original."

"Then have Stephanie write it," Sue said at once. "She always comes up with good ideas."

"The best," Gia agreed.

Stephanie felt herself blushing. "Wow. Thanks, guys!"

Ms. Blith smiled at her. "The vote sounds unanimous. Why don't you try it, Stephanie?"

"I'd love to—" Stephanie began. *But I promised Allie and Darcy that I wouldn't take on any new projects,* she remembered. "But—but I already have a lot going on," she stammered.

"We all do," Sue told her. "But working for the *Scribe* means you're willing to take on extra assignments."

"I know," Stephanie said. *But now is not a good time!* she added to herself.

"Good, then it's settled," Ms. Blith said. "Now, who would like to do a monthly sports interview?"

Stephanie sat back in her chair, feeling dazed. *How did I allow myself to get talked into that?* she wondered. *And what will Darcy and Allie think when they see my name on the byline?*

Stephanie took a deep breath and tried to calm down.

After all, she thought, *it's just one measly column. What's the worst that could happen?*

CHAPTER
3

◆ ◀ ◂ ◆

"Slow down, Comet!" Stephanie called. "I said I'd take you for a walk, not a race!"

The Tanners' big golden retriever didn't even glance back.

Stephanie held on to the long leash and jogged to keep up with her dog. "What are you so excited about?" she asked him.

Ahead of her, Comet's tail waved like a great, golden plume. Maybe he was excited because this was the first time in weeks she'd taken him to Golden Gate Park. Or maybe Comet was just happy because it was a gorgeous fall afternoon.

Or maybe, Stephanie realized, *he's following a scent.* "Please tell me we're not chasing a squirrel," she murmured.

Comet scrambled forward, pulling hard on the leash. He ran toward a young German shepherd and began licking its face.

"Hey, Jackson!" Stephanie said to the shepherd. Then she smiled at the tall boy in glasses who held the dog's leash. "Hi, Billy."

Billy Dean went to Kennedy Middle School, in another part of the city. He and Stephanie became friends when Bingo—the raccoon who was John Muir's mascot—disappeared. The rumor was that some kids from Kennedy stole Bingo. So Stephanie went undercover at Kennedy to investigate.

Even though John Muir and Kennedy were major sports rivals, Stephanie and Billy remained friends. Every so often they'd meet in the park and walk their dogs together.

"What's up, Steph?" Billy asked.

"Too much," Stephanie replied. "I'm behind on my homework, I have to write a new column, and today's my day to walk Comet."

Billy shrugged and smiled. "So let's do it.

"So," he said to Stephanie as they walked, "I know this is a strange question but—are you dating anyone now?"

Stephanie thought about the new boy, Keir. *I wish!* she said silently. But all they'd had was one conversation. That didn't count. Besides, with the Friends First vow, there was no way she would get to date him.

"You're being very silent and mysterious," Billy teased. "That must mean yes."

"Actually, it's no," she replied. "How about you?"

"No one right now," Billy admitted. "But, unfortunately, there's someone who wants to date me."

"What do you mean?" Stephanie asked.

"There's this girl in my class. Her name's Carrie. And I'm ninety-nine percent certain she's going to ask me out."

"If you don't want to go out with her, just say so," Stephanie advised.

"I don't want to hurt her feelings," Billy answered. "Don't get me wrong. Carrie's great. But she reminds me of my nine-year-old sister, and my sister drives me up the wall."

"Yeah, I know all about sisters," Stephanie sympathized.

They were quiet for a moment and then Billy looked at her with a gleam of interest. "Steph, I just had an idea. Friday night a bunch of kids from Kennedy are going to the ice rink. I'm pretty sure Carrie will be there."

"So?"

"So if you came along, and Carrie saw you and me skating together, then she'd figure I was already going out with someone. She'd forget all about me."

"You mean, you want me to *pretend* we're going out?"

"Just for the night," Billy assured her. "You don't go to Kennedy, so Carrie will never know that we're not really a couple. This is so great! She'll give up her crush on me, and I won't have to hurt her feelings."

"I don't know," Stephanie protested. "It sounds awfully complicated."

"It's just so someone nice doesn't get hurt," Billy pointed out. "Think of it as . . . being in a play or something."

Stephanie grinned. "I could get into that."

Billy faced her. "Look, I know what it feels like to ask someone out and get turned down. It happened to me in seventh grade. It made me feel like a total reject!"

Stephanie eyed him skeptically. "You don't look too messed up to me," she said. "Obviously, you recovered."

"That's because I got picked as a starter on the basketball team," Billy told her. "Suddenly lots of girls were interested in me. It's weird how being a jock changes your whole social life. At any rate, will you do it?"

"I can't," she told him. "I'm supposed to go to a sleepover with Darcy and Allie that night."

"What time is the sleepover?" Billy asked.

"Eight," Stephanie replied. "Why?"

"Then this could work!" Billy said excitedly. "The evening skating session at the rink starts at seven-thirty. We could skate for . . . an hour . . . and then my dad could pick us up and drop you at your sleepover. You'd be there by nine, latest."

"I don't know," Stephanie said reluctantly. "I promised Allie and Darcy—"

"You won't be breaking your promise," Billy assured her. "You'll just be missing one little hour of an overnight party. Please—will you at least think about it?"

Stephanie crossed her arms and tried to glare at him. But she couldn't really be angry with Billy. She thought it was sweet that he was trying so hard not to hurt Carrie.

"Besides," Billy went on. "I know that Dana and Sherri and a lot of other kids would love to see you."

Stephanie thought about that. She hadn't seen any of her friends from Kennedy in months.

"Please," Billy said. "You'd be doing me a really *huge* favor."

It's only an hour, Stephanie thought. Darcy and Allie wouldn't mind if she was an hour late. Not if she let them know ahead of time.

"Okay," she said at last. "I'll go skating with you on Friday night. But only until eight-thirty."

Billy grinned. "It's a deal."

Stephanie shook his hand. *After all,* she reasoned, *going out with Billy isn't starting a new project or dating. I'm not really breaking the rules of Friends First.*

Am I?

CHAPTER
4

"Do you notice anything odd?" Stephanie asked.

She, Allie, Darcy, and about a dozen others were gathered in the school gym. It was Thursday afternoon. They were waiting for their first swing class to begin.

Allie glanced around. "You mean, that there are four boys here? I can't believe guys actually signed up for a dance class!"

Darcy grinned. "I told you, swing is hot."

"Well, they're going to make me feel self-conscious," Allie said. "I was sure the class would be all girls."

"It's no big deal," Stephanie decided. "We go to regular dances with guys all the time."

"I guess." Allie didn't sound convinced. "I'm

25

not going to be here for the full hour anyway. I have to leave fifteen minutes early today for a piano lesson."

"Me too," Darcy said. "I mean, not for a piano lesson. My dad got tickets for a WNBA game, and he's picking me up."

Stephanie felt a wave of relief flood through her. She wasn't the only one who had to be flexible about the Friends First commitment. "Well, I can stay for the end of swing class," she said. "But I'll be an hour late for our sleepover tomorrow."

"Steph—" Allie began.

The door to the gym office opened then. A young woman wearing a short, flared skirt and a bright red sweater set walked across the floor. Her long black hair was caught up in a ponytail, and she carried a boom box.

She set down the boom box. "Hi, my name is Liz," she said. "And I see that you all watched the same commercial," she added, laughing. "I'm the only one here who isn't wearing khakis."

She slipped a tape into a cassette player and turned it on. The brassy music of a big band began to fill the gym.

Liz began to tap one soft-soled shoe to the lively rhythm. "Swing is danced to jazz," she went on.

"Another way of looking at it is that swing *is* jazz—it's the way the music would move if it had arms and legs."

Allie shook her head. "I don't know if I'm going to be any good at this," she whispered to Stephanie.

"Why don't you all tap one foot along with me while I talk? Just get the beat for now," Liz urged them.

They all began to tap.

"The main thing about swing dancing is that it's fun," Liz went on. "It's usually danced in couples, and the boy usually leads. But it's good for girls to know how to lead, too."

Liz swayed to the beat of the music, snapping her fingers to the rhythm. "Let's all clap the rhythm. One. Two. Three. Four."

"Come on, Allie," Darcy whispered. "This isn't hard."

"Good." Liz sounded encouraging. "Okay, keep clapping but now march in place in time to the beat. Feel it with your whole body. And now pair off, everyone."

Within seconds Stephanie realized that everyone had a partner except her.

Allie held out her hand. She and Darcy were paired. "Want to be a trio?" she asked Stephanie.

"Sure," Stephanie said.

"We begin to dance swing with a single-step rhythm. Each foot moves on a beat of music," Liz explained. "So leaders start by rocking with your left foot forward, your right foot back. Followers start with the right foot forward. While we're moving, I want you to count, 'slow, slow, rock it' for the quick step."

"Slow, slow, rock it," Stephanie murmured. She smiled as she realized they were all doing a very basic step.

Although she was the shortest, Allie was in the middle, trying to lead. She had her left arm around Darcy and her right around Stephanie. But Stephanie and Darcy had no idea of how to follow Allie. So they all kept jumping back and forth to the beat of the music.

Suddenly Stephanie became aware of a tall, pretty girl at the other end of the gym who was a really good dancer.

"Who's that?" she asked. "I've never seen her before."

"Her name is Marina. She's in my math class," Darcy said. "She just moved here from Wyoming. She seems really nice."

"She's had swing classes before," Allie muttered. "It shows!" Marina led her partner in an underarm turn.

"Let's try that!" Stephanie suggested.

Allie frowned. "I don't know how to make you turn."

"Like this!" Darcy showed her, pulling Allie's arm up and turning under it.

"Ouch!" Allie cried loudly. She twisted around, dragging Stephanie with her.

"Whoops!" Stephanie cried as she tripped over someone's legs.

The next thing she knew, she and Allie and Darcy were sitting in a tangle of arms and legs on the gym floor.

Stephanie, Allie, and Darcy exchanged a quick look. Then they all started giggling.

Liz came over to them. "Are you three okay?" she asked.

"Fine," Stephanie answered.

"Dancing in threes is a little complicated," Liz said, smiling. "Why don't I partner one of you for now?"

She held her hand out to Allie. Allie got up, and Liz showed her how to place her hands. "And slow, slow, rock it!" Liz called out. She began to guide Allie through the steps. "Slow, slow, rock it!"

Stephanie and Darcy began to chant the rhythm as well. The class went by so quickly that Stephanie was surprised when it was time for

Darcy and Allie to leave. But that meant she got to be Liz's partner for the last fifteen minutes of the class.

Liz called out another rhythm, "Slow, slow, quick, quick, slow, slow, rock it!" On the "rock it," she showed Stephanie how to do a little kick.

Stephanie really had to concentrate now. Her feet got a little mixed up, but watching Liz helped.

"This is so cool!" Stephanie said breathlessly.

"It gets better," Liz promised. "Just wait till you have some of the combinations memorized. Then you'll really swing!"

Stephanie imagined herself spinning and doing acrobatic flips—with Keir as her partner.

They stopped dancing as the music stopped. "That's all for today," Liz called out. "I'll see you all next Thursday."

Stephanie and the other girls filed out into the locker room. Marina stood in front of the mirror and ran a brush through her long brown hair.

"Hi," Stephanie said. "My name's Stephanie Tanner. Are you new here?"

"Marina Rees," the girl replied. "My family moved to San Francisco a couple of weeks ago."

"And you've had swing lessons before," Stephanie guessed.

Marina smiled. "In my old school, in Wyoming, a lot of kids were into it. We used to have swing dances every Friday night."

"You mean your whole school took lessons?" Stephanie said. "Wow!" She tried to picture everyone at John Muir dancing swing. Most of the guys in her school had trouble doing the kind of dance where they just stood and bounced a little.

Marina took her backpack from a locker and pulled on a teal fleece jacket. "Let me know if you ever want to practice."

Stephanie hesitated. It would be fun to practice with Marina—but swing class was something that she was doing with Darcy and Allie. She wondered if practicing with Marina broke the rules of Friends First.

"Thanks," Stephanie said. "Maybe I will."

They walked out of the girls' locker room together. Stephanie saw Keir coming out of the boys' locker room. His hair was wet—as if he just showered—and he was carrying a gym bag.

"Hey," Keir called out as he saw them. "Stephanie, I was hoping I'd run into you again." He smiled at Marina. "I'm Keir. I just transferred to John Muir. From Colorado."

Marina smiled back at him. "I just transferred, too. But from Wyoming."

"This is the first time my family's moved," Keir admitted. "It's weird to feel so out of place."

"I know what you mean," Marina said. "I keep looking around for the Tetons."

"That's how I feel about the Rockies," Keir told her.

Stephanie suddenly felt left out of their conversation. *It's ridiculous to feel jealous,* Stephanie told herself sternly. *You barely know Keir. So what if he and Marina have something in common?* Still, she couldn't help wanting to change the subject.

"So," Stephanie said to Keir, "you look like you just came from some sort of team practice."

"Soccer. I made the team here. What about you?"

"We took a swing class," Stephanie answered.

Keir winced. "I'm the world's worst dancer," he confessed.

"I could teach you," Marina offered.

"Thanks but no thanks," Keir told her. "Dribbling a soccer ball is about as coordinated as I get. I don't think I'm ready to push my luck."

Marina's hazel eyes widened as she saw a clock on the wall. "I can't believe it!" she said. "It's almost four forty-five. And I've got to take my lit-

32

tle sister for a swimming lesson at five. I've got to run!"

Marina rushed off.

Keir grinned at Stephanie. "So . . . are you busy Friday night? I was hoping you'd go to a movie with me."

Stephanie felt her heart speed up—Keir was asking her out on a date!

Then she felt her heart slow again—as she realized she had to say no. Friday night was the night she was going skating with Billy and then to the sleepover.

"I'm sorry," she said.

She saw a flash of disappointment in Keir's blue eyes. They were almost the exact same shade of dusky blue, she realized, as his fleece jacket.

"Oh—I guess you're already going out with someone," he said.

"I'm not," Stephanie said quickly. "I mean, that's not the reason. It's just that I already have plans for Friday."

"How about Saturday?" Keir asked.

"Saturday would be—" Stephanie was about to say "great." And then she remembered her vow. "Just as bad," she finished. "I'm sorry. This whole week is pretty booked."

"No big deal," Keir said. "Maybe another time."

"Sure," Stephanie replied. But her heart was sinking. She'd promised her friends not to date. For one whole month!

Stephanie remembered the way Keir had smiled at Marina. *Maybe Keir is interested in me now*, she thought.

But will he still be interested one month from now— if I keep turning him down?

CHAPTER
5

◆ ◀ ◂ ◆

Danny Tanner pulled his car into the parking lot behind the skating rink. "So you're sure you've got a ride to Allie's tonight?" he asked Stephanie.

"Billy's dad will pick us up at eight-thirty and then drop me at the sleepover," Stephanie answered.

"That sounds good," her father told her. "Because I'm meeting Joey, Becky, and Jesse at the museum for the media series. None of us will be around to give you a ride."

Danny and Becky were cohosts and coproducers of the TV show, *Wake Up, San Francisco*. Jesse and Joey cohosted a local radio show. All four were attending a series of lectures on media in the Bay Area. Fortunately, that evening D.J. had agreed to stay home to watch Michelle and the twins.

"It's no problem, Dad," Stephanie assured him. "I've got it covered."

He leaned forward and kissed her forehead. "Okay, sweetie. Have fun. I'll see you in the morning."

" 'Night, Dad," Stephanie said. "And thanks for the ride."

Stephanie entered the rink, her white figure skates slung over her shoulder. She was wearing close-fitting jeans and an oversize white sweater. Her long blond hair was pulled back in a French braid.

She sat down on the bleachers, took off her boots, and began putting on her skates. She was lacing them up when Billy Dean walked up to her. "It's my skating partner," he said happily. He sat down beside her. "Hey, Steph, thanks for coming."

Stephanie glanced around. It was early in the evening. The ice was still fairly empty and smooth. Skaters were arriving in small groups of two and three. She didn't recognize anyone from Kennedy besides Billy.

"Is Carrie here yet?" Stephanie whispered.

"Not yet, but she will be."

Billy changed into a pair of scuffed black hockey skates and led the way out onto the ice. A Backstreet Boys song was playing on the speaker system. Stephanie let herself glide to the familiar music. Billy matched his pace to hers. He was a good skater, she realized, graceful and rhythmic.

Billy skated closer to her. "Don't look now," he whispered. "But on the other side of the rink, there's a girl wearing white tights and a short pink skirt."

"Carrie?" Stephanie guessed.

Billy nodded.

"She's really pretty!" Stephanie said.

"Yeah, she is," Billy agreed. "Just not my type."

Billy smiled. He glanced back toward Carrie as a slower tune played. "Steph, would you mind holding hands for a few minutes?"

Stephanie held out her hand. Billy took it and pulled her into a gentle spin. Then they skated side by side in sync. *It's sort of weird to be holding hands with Billy*, Stephanie thought. She noticed Carrie frown as she passed them.

"Hey, stranger!"

Stephanie glanced toward the wall that edged the rink and saw two of her friends from Kennedy. She waved and skated over to them.

Dana Pugnosian and Sherri Ruiz rushed

toward Stephanie. Dana reached over the wall and hugged her.

"We haven't seen you in months!" Dana said.

"I know. My life's been pretty crazed," Stephanie explained. "How about you guys? It's so good to see you again."

"We've been pretty busy, too," Sherri said. "Dana and I are helping out at a wildlife shelter."

"So what are you doing in this end of town?" Dana asked.

Billy skated up to them. "She's here with me," he answered.

Dana's blue eyes lit up. "I knew you two would be great together," she said. "I've been trying to match you up since the first time we met."

"We—" Stephanie began, but Billy cut her off.

"We really haven't been going out very long," he said quickly. "Actually," he went on, "tonight's the first time."

"Then we'll leave you alone," Dana said. "But I know Laura and Scott and everyone would love to see you, Steph. Will you be at the Kennedy dance next Friday?"

Billy shot Stephanie a questioning look. "Uh . . . sure," he answered.

"But—" Stephanie began.

"Great, because we have a special gift for you,"

Dana said, interrupting her. "Actually, we've got gifts for Allie and Darcy, too."

"Gifts?" Stephanie asked. "What are they?"

"You'll see next Friday," Sherri promised. "Catch you then.

"Stephanie turned to Billy as the two girls from Kennedy began skating. "Why did you tell them we were going out?" she demanded.

"Carrie was skating by," Billy explained. "I didn't want her to overhear me saying we're just friends."

"Well, then why didn't you tell them the truth when Carrie was out of earshot?"

"You could have said something, too," Billy pointed out.

"I didn't want to contradict you!"

Billy did a slow spin on the ice, then turned to face her. "You know, Steph, maybe you should come to the dance next week. Dana's right. A lot of kids at Kennedy would love to see you."

"And then Carrie would have no doubt that you're taken," Stephanie added.

"It's not that," Billy told her. "We don't even have to go as a couple. There's a great band from the high school that's going to play. Plus Dana has those presents for you. It will be fun."

It probably would, Stephanie thought. *And I'm*

certainly not going to be dating for a while. I might as well have a good time.

"All right," she told Billy. "We're on for the dance next Friday'night. But after that, *no more* pretend dates."

"Fair enough," Billy agreed. He nodded toward Carrie. She was skating hand in hand with a boy with wavy blond hair. "I think she got the message. I really owe you for this."

Suddenly Stephanie remembered what she had to do *this* Friday night. She glanced at the clock. It was eight twenty-eight. "Isn't your dad supposed to be here soon?" she asked Billy.

Billy checked the clock, too. "Yeah. He should be here any minute. We'd better get off the ice."

The two of them changed back into their shoes. Stephanie stood up and wriggled her toes. It felt good to no longer be balancing on metal blades.

"We should wait by the front door," Billy said.

Stephanie tied her skates together, put on her jacket and scarf, and followed Billy outside. A thick fog hung over the city. Even the nearby lights in the parking lot seemed dim.

Ten minutes later she looked at her watch. "It's almost a quarter of nine. I wonder where your dad is. Do you think he forgot us?"

"Not possible," Billy assured her. "My dad is Mr. Conscientious. He'll be here any minute now."

"I'd better call Allie's house and warn her that I'm going to be late," Stephanie said.

"That's probably a good idea," Billy agreed. "The pay phones are near the snack bar."

Back inside the building Stephanie found the three pay phones. She dropped some coins into the first one and waited for the dial tone. Nothing.

Stephanie pressed the coin return and put her money in again. Again no dial tone. This time when she tried to get her change back, nothing came out.

With a sigh Stephanie stepped over to the next phone. She put in more coins and waited. Again there was no dial tone. No sound at all.

I can't believe this! Stephanie thought.

She tried the third phone—with the exact same result!

Stephanie ran back outside. She found Billy leaning against the brick wall of the building, his hands in his pockets.

"No sign of your dad?" she asked.

"Not yet. What did Allie say?"

"I couldn't get her," Stephanie explained. "All of the pay phones are dead." She checked her watch and groaned. "I'm supposed to be at Allie's house in five minutes!"

"Maybe someone at the rink will let you use their phone," Billy suggested.

"Good plan," Stephanie said. She dashed back inside and went up to the desk. "Could I make a quick local call?" she asked. "I tried all three pay phones, and they're all broken."

"The pay phones are fine," the man behind the desk told her. "But there's a cable down. All the phones in this area are out. The phone company says they won't be working until tomorrow."

"Well, that explains it," Stephanie said. "Thanks."

Stephanie went back outside. She found Billy sitting on the ground. "This is a disaster," she reported. "None of the phones is working. Allie and Darcy will think I stood them up."

"Look, it's not your fault," Billy reminded her. "Besides, they're your friends. They'll understand."

"I hope so," Stephanie said.

At eleven-fifteen that evening Mr. Dean's car finally pulled up in front of the rink.

"Dad!" Billy said. "Are you all right?"

"I'm fine," his father answered. "But when I

was coming back from your uncle's house in Berkeley, Highway 80 was backed up for miles. Then there was a bad accident on the bridge into the city, and I sat at the tollbooth for over an hour!"

Mr. Dean smiled at Stephanie. "I'm sorry, Stephanie. I know you wanted to be at your friend's house by nine."

Stephanie tried not to act upset. She knew it wasn't Mr. Dean's fault that she couldn't make it to the sleepover.

Stephanie shrugged. "It's kind of late to show up there now," she said. "Could you take me home instead?"

"No problem," he replied. "That is, unless we hit traffic."

Twenty minutes later Stephanie was safely home. She looked at her watch. It was nearly midnight, way too late to call Allie's. She would just have to talk to Allie and Darcy tomorrow.

I hope they're not too unhappy that I didn't show up, Stephanie thought. *I'll just have to make it up to them—somehow.*

CHAPTER
6

◆ ◀ ◆ ◆

Stephanie woke up at eight on Saturday morning. Michelle was already out of bed. For once Stephanie had their room to herself. She put on a long-sleeved powder blue T-shirt and her favorite overalls. Then she brushed out her hair and studied herself in the mirror.

"I look like a decent person and a trustworthy friend," she reassured herself. "And last night I really tried hard to let Allie and Darcy know what was happening. So why do I feel like a total creep?"

"Because you're nuts," Michelle answered cheerfully. She walked into their room and dropped down on her bed. "Talking to yourself is not a good sign. I'm starting to worry about you."

Stephanie laughed. "I'll be better soon—I promise," she said. She went downstairs and found Danny, Jesse, and the twins at the kitchen table eating breakfast.

Her father gave her a questioning look. "I thought you were at Allie's."

"I was supposed to be," Stephanie said. She explained what had happened the night before. "So I want to go over there now and explain to Darcy and Allie," she finished.

"Don't you want to eat first?" Uncle Jesse asked. "I made my special ham and cheese omelette."

Nicky used his fork to lift up a string of melted cheddar. "It's gooey," he told Stephanie.

Stephanie smiled at him. "It looks good and gooey," she said. "Just the way I like it. But I really have to talk to Darcy and Allie now."

"Go ahead," her father told her. "Just make sure you eat something soon."

"I will," Stephanie promised.

She grabbed her jacket and started out. She felt grateful that her dad hadn't made her eat breakfast. The sooner she got over to Allie's, the better she'd feel.

"Stephanie!" Mrs. Taylor answered the door. She was wearing her fuzzy red bathrobe. "Where have you been? Allie and Darcy were worried about you."

"I came to explain," Stephanie said. "Are they up yet?"

Allie's mother smiled. "They're in the living room, eating French toast and watching cartoons. Would you like some French toast?"

"Maybe later," Stephanie said. "Thanks."

Stephanie headed into the Taylors' cozy living room. She found Darcy stretched out on the couch. Allie was curled up in the big easy chair.

" 'Morning, everyone," Stephanie said.

Allie blinked and sat up in her chair. "Steph, are you okay? What happened to you last night?"

Darcy reached for the remote and flicked off the TV. "We were worried about you. You said you'd be an hour late. Not that you'd show up the next morning."

"I know." Stephanie sat down in the rocking chair. "And I'm really sorry. I tried to call you, but—" Stephanie explained what had happened at the skating rink the night before.

Darcy looked thoughtful. "You know, originally, I was supposed to shoot baskets with Josh last night. But you were the one who told me to cancel it. For Friends First. How come you didn't do the same thing with Billy Dean?"

"Because I thought I could do both things," Stephanie said honestly. "I had it all planned. I'd be at the rink until eight-thirty, and then I'd be here at nine. I was only going to be one teensy hour late!"

Allie crossed her arms over her chest. "I thought one of the rules of Friends First was no dating for the next month."

"Skating with Billy was *not* a date," Stephanie told them. "I was just helping him out."

"It's great that you're so concerned about Billy's friends," Darcy said, "but what about—"

Wow, they really are mad! Stephanie thought.

The phone rang. Mrs. Taylor called out, "Allie, it's for you!"

To Stephanie's surprise Allie looked nervous for a second. "Could you take a message, Mom?" she called back hurriedly. She turned to Stephanie. "Friends First," she said as if proving her point.

"See?" Darcy added.

"I see," Stephanie said. "You're right. Both of you."

Allie's green eyes softened. "Come on, Darce," she said. "It's not Stephanie's fault that Billy's dad got stuck in traffic. Or that the phones were out."

"I know that," Darcy said. "But what's the point of Friends First if you put your best friends second?"

Allie gave Stephanie a sympathetic look. "She has a point."

Stephanie took a deep breath. "Okay," she said. "I shouldn't have scheduled anything when we had a sleepover planned. I promise I won't do anything like that again. Okay?"

"That sounds good to me," Allie said.

"Me too," Darcy agreed. "Sorry I gave you such a hard time."

"Guys," Stephanie said, "there's something I need to tell you."

Darcy took a sip of her orange juice. "Speak," she joked.

Stephanie suddenly felt shy. "I know we agreed to no dating for a month," she began. "And that's probably a good idea. But I just met this guy at school. His name is Keir Cooper."

"The new kid from Colorado?" Allie asked.

Stephanie nodded.

"He's adorable!" Allie said.

"I know," Stephanie agreed. "And he's asked me out twice now. Each time I've said no. Because of Friends First. The thing is, I really like him, and

48

I'm afraid that if I keep saying no, he'll ask someone else out."

"So what are you saying?" Darcy asked.

"Well . . ." Stephanie hesitated. She had to choose her words carefully. "We set up pretty strict rules. I was thinking, maybe we could let ourselves have one exception each."

"You already had yours. Last night," Darcy pointed out. She shook her head, and her black braids swirled around her head. "I'm not trying to be mean here, Steph. It's just that if we keep making exceptions, then we'll be exactly where we were when we started Friends First."

"I agree," Allie said. "After all, the rules are just for one month to get our friendship back on track."

Stephanie couldn't argue with that. And even if she did argue, she was totally outnumbered.

She was also feeling a little guilty. She hadn't even told them about her *Scribe* column or the Kennedy dance. The truth was, she didn't want one exception. She wanted half a dozen.

Allie stood up and stretched. "This has gotten too serious," she declared. "I say it's time we have some fun."

"What do you have in mind?" Darcy asked.

Allie walked over to the CD player and slipped

in a disc. She began to snap her fingers to the big band music that played. "Slow, slow, rock it!" she called out. She began doing one of the basic swing steps.

"Slow, slow, rock it!" Stephanie and Darcy chanted as they joined her.

For a while Stephanie forgot about her complicated life. She just concentrated on dancing and having fun with her friends.

Later, as Stephanie started back home, her worry returned. Her best friends were no longer angry with her—which was good. And they'd just had a great time dancing together—also good.

So why didn't she feel better about Friends First? Why was she still so confused?

CHAPTER
7

◆ ◀ ◆ ◆

Stephanie hurried into the weekly *Scribe* meeting. For once she was on time. She took a seat next to Sue Kramer.

"Hi," Sue said. "How's it going?"

"Okay," Stephanie answered. "How about you?"

Sue pulled two neatly typed pages from a neon-pink folder. "I was up until ten last night, writing my first review," she explained. "But at least it's done."

Terrific, Stephanie thought. *Sue's already finished her column. And I don't even know what I'm going to write about.*

Ms. Blith clapped her hands together. "All right, everyone," she said. "Today's meeting is basically a progress report. Next week I'll ask you to start submitting your articles for the new pages. Sue, why don't you begin?"

"On Sunday I went to the new animated movie," Sue said. "The one about toads. It was totally hilarious. So I wrote it up last night." She handed Ms. Blith her review.

"Anyone else?" Ms. Blith asked.

Gia raised her hand. "I put up flyers, saying we wanted candid photos," she reported. "Look what's already come in."

She offered Ms. Blith an envelope filled with photographs.

The teacher glanced through them quickly. "These are terrific," she said. "It's going to be hard to choose just one."

Quentin Baglio held up a folder that was nearly as thick as the San Francisco phone book. "I started printing out the best kids' web pages," he said. "My problem is that there's so much to write about, I don't know where to start."

I should have problems like that! Stephanie thought.

Sue Kramer said Quentin should just focus on one web site per column. Bill Klepper thought Quentin should focus on a different topic each time. Tiffany said he should write about the sites with the coolest graphics.

Stephanie couldn't concentrate on Quentin's problem. She was too busy worrying about her own. What was she going to write about? It had to be something personal, and at the same time, something that everyone could relate to. Hastily she scribbled a list.

"So, Stephanie," Ms. Blith said at last. "Have you had any ideas for your first column?"

"Um . . . only a few," Stephanie replied.

"Why don't you try them out on us?" the adviser suggested.

Stephanie glanced at her list:

Things You Learn Walking to School
The Color of Classroom Walls Really Makes a
   Difference
We Could All Use a Better PA System

She groaned inwardly. Each idea seemed lamer than the one before.

"Stephanie?" Ms. Blith prompted her.

Stephanie cleared her throat. "I was thinking," she began, "about walking to school every day."

"Sounds exciting to me," Bill joked.

Stephanie glared at him. "When you walk to school, you really learn a lot about your neighborhood," she went on. "And . . . the seasons. And also, it's a really good time to think about your classes and your friends."

"Maybe," Tiffany objected, "but over half the student body gets here on school buses. So that wouldn't really apply to them."

"True," Sue agreed. "Any other ideas?"

Stephanie glanced at the second item on her list. "I was thinking about the art room. You know how Ms. Delgatto painted that one wall purple and all the cabinets deep red? Well, I think those colors make everyone feel more creative. All the other classrooms are boring white or that sickly green . . ."

"The art room looks great," Sue spoke up. "But what really makes a difference is the teacher. Not the color of the room."

"Definitely," Quentin agreed. "Besides, who wants to read about walls?" He rolled his eyes.

So much for that idea, Stephanie thought.

"Anything else, Stephanie?" Ms. Blith asked. Stephanie could hear the impatience in her voice.

Stephanie glanced at her last topic and decided she didn't want to hear what everyone thought about the PA system. "No, not really," she murmured. "But I'm still working on it."

Stephanie left the *Scribe* meeting feeling discouraged. She put on her jacket and walked down the empty hallways toward the exit.

What's wrong with me? she wondered. *I used to be creative, imaginative. Now I just feel like a dud.*

"We meet again," said a familiar voice.

Stephanie looked up and felt her heart skip a beat. It was Keir, coming out of another soccer practice. Or at least out of another shower. His hair was wet and slicked back, and he was carrying that gym bag again.

"More soccer practice?" Stephanie asked.

"Yup. How about you?"

"*Scribe* meeting," Stephanie answered. "How was soccer?"

"Pathetic," Keir admitted. "We had a scrimmage, and my team not only lost, we actually kicked the ball straight through the other team's goalposts."

Stephanie slid her backpack onto her shoulders. "Then you're doing about as well as I am," she said. "I had to come up with ideas for a column. And my first two were totally rejected."

"What about your third idea?" Keir asked.

Stephanie grimaced. "That one was so bad, I didn't have the nerve to bring it up."

Keir's blue eyes narrowed. "How bad could an idea be?"

"Terrible," Stephanie assured him. "Take my word for it."

Keir started walking toward the exit, and Stephanie fell in beside him. She felt comfortable walking with Keir. As if they were already really good friends instead of two people who barely knew each other.

"So," Keir said, "what is this column supposed to be about?"

"That's the problem," Stephanie explained. "I have no idea. It's supposed to be about school but also be personal. Something everyone can relate to."

"Like, how you love buying covers for your textbooks?" Keir joked.

Stephanie shrugged. "That topic is about as good as mine."

Keir winced. "I do see why you're stuck."

He pushed open the door that led outside. The earthy scent of damp leaves mixed with the aroma of freshly baked bread from the new bakery down the street.

The air was chilly. Stephanie rubbed her hands together briskly, then crossed her arms and tucked them under her armpits for warmth. She wished she had her gloves.

"Where are you headed?" Keir asked.

Stephanie nodded toward the bus stop. "I'm going to catch the late bus." She looked at her watch, then added, "Though it won't leave for another twenty minutes."

"Oh." Keir glanced toward the bakery. "You want a sticky bun? We could eat them while you wait for the bus."

Stephanie smiled at Keir. "That sounds good," she said.

"Great," he said, and started walking toward the bakery. "Now let's solve your problem. We need a topic that everyone can relate to. . . . Let's see . . . I think you should write about . . . writing difficult columns."

"Everyone would say that's not relevant," Stephanie said. "After all, not that many kids write for the *Scribe*."

"Yeah, but we all have homework assignments that leave us totally uninspired," Keir pointed out. "It's the same thing. Except homework is worse, because you get graded on it."

"True," Stephanie agreed. "But somehow writing a column on writing a column doesn't sound too exciting."

"Right. You need exciting," Keir said. "How about . . . a column about fighting crime at John Muir Middle School?"

"What crime?" Stephanie asked.

Keir grinned. "No crime? Okay, scratch that. I

know! You can write about how you discovered this secret locker that allows students to time travel into the school's past. You step inside, and the next thing you know, you're in nineteen ninety-one, taking some old test that you never studied for."

"Actually, the last time I tried time travel," Stephanie joked, "I got stuck in the secret locker for three hours with a pair of really smelly sneakers."

"Not good column material," Keir decided. He opened the door to the bakery, and a string of brass bells rang gently. The warm, sweet scent of freshly baked pastries surrounded them. They studied the glass case filled with rows of baked goods.

"You don't have to have a sticky bun," Keir assured her. "If you'd rather have a brownie or a doughnut or—"

"No, I'll have a sticky bun, please," Stephanie told the gray-haired woman behind the counter.

"Make that two," Keir said. He looked at the hot cocoa machine in the corner. "And two cups of cocoa, please."

They took their cocoa and pastries and went out into the cold. Stephanie sipped her cocoa as they started back toward the bus stop. "This is perfect," she said. "Thanks."

"No problem," Keir said. "It's not every day I

58

meet someone who knows about the secret time-travel locker."

Stephanie laughed. She was having fun goofing around with Keir. She felt disappointed when she saw the late bus parked at the bus stop.

Keir noticed the bus, too. "Before you go," he said, "I wanted to ask you . . ."

"Yes?" Stephanie said.

Keir sounded a little nervous. "I have two tickets for next Friday night's Iguanas concert. Would you go with me?"

"The Iguanas?" Stephanie asked in disbelief. The Iguanas were an incredibly hot band from New Orleans. "How did you get tickets to that? They've been sold out for months."

"My mom," Keir explained. "She does consulting for their manager. She set up the software that books their tours."

"That is so cool!" Stephanie said.

Keir grinned. "Yeah, my parents aren't totally hopeless, I guess. So . . . do you want to go to the concert?"

"Yes!" Then Stephanie remembered. Friday night was the Kennedy dance. Besides, even if she were free, going out with Keir meant breaking the Friends First vow.

She felt her face redden. This was so awkward.

She really liked Keir, and she had to turn him down. Again. "I mean, no. I can't," she said quickly. "I mean, I've already got something I've got to do on Friday night."

"You *are* going out with someone else," Keir said.

"No," Stephanie told him. "I'm not. Really." She studied his face. Keir seemed disappointed and confused. She really liked him. She needed to tell him the truth.

"It's like this," she said slowly. "I made a promise to my two best friends."

"What kind of promise?" he asked.

"See, Darcy and Allie and I realized we weren't making time to get together," Stephanie began. "And we used to do *everything* together. It was like we were losing our friendship. So we promised that, for the next month, none of us would take on any new activities or date anyone. Just for a month . . . until we got things back on track." She looked at Keir hopefully. "Do you understand?"

"Not really," Keir answered. "I mean, if you're really friends, then you don't have to worry about not seeing each other. You'll still be friends whenever you do get together."

Stephanie hadn't expected Keir to argue with her. Clearly, he didn't get it.

"It wouldn't be the same," she explained. "Last

weekend Darcy and her family went to Chicago because her grandmother was sick. And I didn't even know about it."

"So?"

"So we're missing out on sharing each other's lives!" Stephanie said.

Keir looked annoyed. "Well, I'm missing out on sharing the lives of *all* my friends in Boulder," he informed her. "And you don't see me vowing not to date or do anything new in my life."

"That's different because you moved," Stephanie shot back.

"It is *not* different!" Keir insisted. "It's just harder because my best friends are over a thousand miles away! But I know that whenever I go back there, they'll still be my friends. And I won't have to make any stupid promises!"

"It is *not* stupid," Stephanie said between her teeth.

"Only the dumbest one I ever heard," Keir retorted. He wheeled around and walked away from the bus.

Stephanie felt as if she might scream in frustration. *Keir has absolutely no right to call my vow dumb!* she thought angrily.

But the trouble is—he might be right!

CHAPTER
8

◆ ◀ ✦ ◆

"Shoop bop a loo bop, a shoop bop a loo—" Allie sang.

Darcy smiled over Allie's head at Stephanie. "Think she liked swing class today?"

Allie snapped her fingers in time to her tune. "Shoop bop a loo bop . . ." She stopped, frowned, corrected the rhythm, and began practicing a step combination.

"Just a little," Stephanie answered Darcy. "It's not every day you see Allie Taylor dancing down the sidewalks."

"I know," Darcy mused. "Kind of reminds me of a really corny old musical."

Allie stopped dancing and glared at her friends. "I just want to practice the combination before I forget it," she said. "After all, John Muir is going to have its first swing dance a week from Saturday. That's only ten days away, and I want to be prepared!"

"What's the big deal?" Stephanie asked. "You'll be as well prepared as anyone else in our swing class."

"Except Marina," Darcy added.

Marina. Stephanie had tried hard not to think about the new girl. But on Wednesday morning—the morning after her argument with Keir—she saw Marina talking to him at his locker.

"She's too tall for him," Stephanie muttered.

"Who's too tall for whom?" Allie wondered. "Who are you talking about?"

"No one," Stephanie said quickly. "I—"

"I can't believe I forgot to tell you!" Darcy broke in suddenly. "Sorry, Steph, it's just that I keep forgetting and if I don't say something now—"

"Tell us already!" Allie demanded.

"This weekend my dad was cleaning out the attic, and he found an old camera bag of his. It was filled with rolls of film that he shot but never developed. So he took them in to the film place and picked them up last night."

"And?" Stephanie asked.

"And he's got photographs of the three of us

going back to sixth grade!" Darcy said. "Allie, do you remember that pink fluffy coat you used to wear?"

Allie groaned. "Not that, please!"

Stephanie laughed, remembering. "I'd love to see a picture of you in that coat. I always thought it made you look like a pink bunny rabbit!"

Allie shut her eyes. "Darce, do you think that if I paid your dad enough money, he'd burn those pictures?"

"Not a chance," Darcy assured her. "But don't worry. He's got some really goofy ones of me in that purple jumpsuit I was so crazy about. And, Steph, he's got one of you right after Allie decided she was going to be a hairstylist."

Stephanie and Allie looked at each other and doubled over, laughing.

"That was the worst haircut of my entire life!" Stephanie gasped.

"Well, it was my first one," Allie defended herself. "I still needed some practice."

"*Some* practice?" Stephanie echoed. "Wasn't that when your mom decided to hide the scissors?"

"Right," Darcy agreed. "And there's another picture that's to die for. Remember in sixth grade when we came up with that Girl Power slogan?"

"Girls together, girls having fun, girls to the rescue, Girl Power, everyone!" the three friends chanted.

Stephanie cracked up again. "Man, someone should have given us a prize for the worst rhyme ever!" she said.

"It wasn't the rhyme that was so bad." Allie giggled. "It was those hokey Girl Power costumes we wore for Halloween."

"They weren't hokey," Stephanie argued. "We just wanted to be superheroes."

"Or fashion disasters," Darcy added, laughing. Her dark eyes lit up with excitement. "Hey, I've got an idea. Why don't you two come over to my house after dinner? I'll make some popcorn, and we can go through all the photographs together."

"That'd be great!" Allie said.

Stephanie felt a twinge of disappointment. "I'd love to," she said, "but I can't. I've got a biology test tomorrow."

"Well, we're not going to look at them without you," Allie said loyally. "Why don't we do a sleepover tomorrow night instead?"

"Perfect," Darcy said. "That way we'll have plenty of time to look at the photos. Maybe we can even make a special scrapbook for them."

"I think D.J. has an extra photo album," Stephanie said excitedly. "There was a special sale at the mall, and she wound up buying two and getting one free. Maybe she'll let us use it."

"And we should write captions underneath the photos," Allie added. "Saying which grade we were in and at whose house and stuff."

"I've already got the first caption," Stephanie joked. *"Haircut by Allie."*

"And for the one of Allie in her coat getting into my dad's car—*The Pink Bunny Rabbit Rides Again!"* Darcy added.

Allie gave her friends a mock frown. "Very funny," she said. "I'll see you two tomorrow. And be prepared—I'm going to think up some captions of my own!"

Allie and Darcy turned toward the street that led to their houses. Stephanie continued toward her house by herself. She smiled as she thought about the photographs. If they were half as ridiculous as they sounded, they'd be a lot of fun to look at. The three of them would have to make another vow, though—not to use them to blackmail each other.

"Stephanie Tanner, how've you been?"

Stephanie looked up to see a slender young woman with close-cropped blond hair. Kendra Davis, a twenty-four-year-old actress, lived across the street from the Tanners.

"I'm doing okay," Stephanie said. "How about you?"

"Still making commercials," Kendra answered. "Last week I was a teenager with bad breath, a talking computer chip, and a rebellious potato that did not want to become a french fry."

"Cool!" Stephanie said.

"It's mostly a lot of waiting around," Kendra confessed. "And memorizing dopey scripts. But I figure it's all good experience. One day someone will let me be a real actress."

"I keep watching for you on TV," Stephanie said. "Do you think those commercials will be on soon?"

"The bad breath one might be," Kendra answered. "But the other two were made for foreign markets. I'll tell you what . . . one day you can come over, and I'll show you the videos."

"I'll be there!" Stephanie promised.

"The parts of a flower include the petals, anther, sepals, stigma, and stamen," Stephanie murmured.

She marked the diagram on her worksheet. "These are definitely the petals, and these are the sepals. And I think that's a stigma. Or is it an anther?" Stephanie opened her textbook with a sigh. Why was she having so much trouble memorizing this stuff?

She was grateful when she heard the phone ringing. Anything to distract her from science, and from the fact that she and Keir weren't speaking.

"I'll get it!" she called, and raced out of her room into the hall.

"Tanner residence," she said into the receiver.

"Hey, Steph," said Billy Dean's friendly voice. "I just called to remind you about the Kennedy dance. And to make sure you had a ride."

"If you're offering me another ride with your dad—"

"Actually my older brother volunteered," Billy said. "And he promised he would definitely *not* go to Berkeley first. So how about it?"

Stephanie smiled. "I guess I really ought to give you a second chance."

"You won't regret it," Billy promised. "The band that's going to play tomorrow night is the best."

"Tomorrow night?" Stephanie echoed. She suddenly felt sick to her stomach.

"Yeah. Tomorrow. Friday night. You said you'd go last Friday, remember?"

"I remember." Stephanie hit her forehead with

the heel of her hand. "Only I totally forgot this afternoon when I agreed to another sleepover with Allie and Darcy. Billy, I can't go."

Billy sighed. "I've got a problem, Stephanie. I didn't want to tell you, but Carrie didn't take the hint last week. She asked me to the dance—and I lied and said I already had a date. So—"

"So you want me to help you out again," Stephanie said slowly.

"Please?" Billy asked. "I was sort of counting on you."

Stephanie thought about it. Darcy and Allie were counting on her, too.

"Plus Dana is bringing those presents for you and Allie and Darcy," he reminded her.

"Oh, right." Stephanie had forgotten about the presents.

"Look," Billy said, "why don't you tell Allie and Darcy the truth—that you already have plans. After all, you agreed to go to the Kennedy dance last Friday."

"That's true," Stephanie said. "I did tell Dana and Sherri I'd be there."

Besides, Stephanie reasoned, Allie and Darcy left swing class early when they had other things to do, and no one had a cow over that. Plus there were the presents to consider.

"And," Billy added, "the three of you can reschedule a sleepover, but I can't exactly reschedule this dance."

"Okay," Stephanie said at last. "I'll talk to them."

"Great," Billy said. "Me and my brother will pick you up tomorrow night at seven."

"Great," Stephanie said. But her stomach was churning as she hung up and dialed Darcy's number.

"Hi, Steph," Darcy said when she picked up the phone. "Did you ask D.J. about that spare photo album?"

"Um—no, I forgot," Stephanie answered honestly. "But I'll ask her as soon as we hang up. It's just that first I have to tell you that I can't come to the sleepover tomorrow night."

"Excuse me?" Darcy said.

"I can't come tomorrow night," Stephanie repeated. It sounded worse every time she said it. "I got so enthusiastic when we were talking about the photos and all, that I totally forgot I already had plans."

"You keep agreeing to spend time with Allie and me and then canceling on us," Darcy said. "It's turning into a pattern."

"It is *not*," Stephanie insisted. "It's more like . . .a freak coincidence. I just—"

"Hold on," Darcy interrupted. "That's my call waiting."

Stephanie waited as Darcy took the other call.

Seconds later Darcy was back on the line. "Sorry, that call . . . it's for my mother. I've got to go. I'll let Allie know about the sleepover, and we'll see you in school tomorrow," she finished.

"But—" Stephanie protested.

" 'Bye." Darcy hung up.

Stephanie stared at the phone receiver in dismay. "Good going, Steph," she muttered to herself. Her life was much too complicated—and it was all her fault!

CHAPTER
9

♦ ◄ ✦ ♦

It was Friday evening, and surprisingly warm for November. Stephanie wore a close-fitting lavender scoop-neck T-shirt, baggy gray cargo pants, and a silver choker. One step ahead of her, Billy Dean led the way into Kennedy Middle School.

"Ready for the best band in San Francisco?" Billy asked.

"Totally ready," she answered. "I could use some fun in my life."

Stephanie felt a lot better. Today at school she worked things out with Allie and Darcy. It helped that Darcy also had to cancel. Something with her parents, she said. Stephanie hadn't asked for more of an explanation. "Look, I understand," she told Darcy. Allie was okay with it, too.

So at least I'm going out, and I don't feel like I'm betraying Friends First! Stephanie thought.

The only problem is that Keir thinks I'm an idiot, she reminded herself. She wouldn't think about that now. Tonight she was just going to have fun.

As they neared the gym, Stephanie could hear the sounds of a band tuning up—guitars, a bass, and drums. Billy immediately began playing air drums. He mimicked the beat so perfectly that Stephanie started laughing.

"You sure you're not with the band?" she asked.

Billy grinned. "I wish," he said as he opened the gym door.

"Stephanie!" Scott, the captain of Kennedy's basketball team and Dana's boyfriend, gave her a hug. "Great to see you!"

"Great to see your T-shirt," Stephanie mumbled into his chest. Scott was so tall that the top of her head didn't even reach his shoulders.

"Sorry." He released her, and Stephanie found herself surrounded by Dana, Sherri, Maria, and Malcolm.

"Billy told us you had trouble getting home from the rink last week," Dana said.

The lead guitarist stepped up to the microphone then and cleared his throat. "Hello, Kennedy!" he said. "We're going to play some music for you tonight, and see if we can make this place jump!" He hit a chord on his guitar and the rest of the band joined in. They played fast and loud, with an irresistible beat.

Billy took Stephanie's hand. "May I have this dance?" he shouted over the music.

"Absolutely!" Stephanie shouted back.

She and Billy began to dance alongside Dana and Scott. Both boys were good dancers. Stephanie was relieved not to have to worry about swing steps and turns for once. She let her body move to the beat. She felt as though the music were rippling right through her.

The band's second song was even better. This time Malcolm, Maria, Sherri, Billy, and Stephanie all danced together in a loose circle. Billy and Malcolm faced each other and added layup and behind-the-back dribbling moves to their dancing. They looked kind of goofy, but they kept the beat perfectly. Stephanie and Sherri laughed, working hard to keep up with the boys.

At one point Billy nodded to his left. Stephanie smiled when she saw Carrie and the blond-haired boy from the skating rink dancing together.

By the fifth song Stephanie was starting to feel a little tired, but they all kept dancing right through the very last song. She couldn't remember the last time she'd had so much fun.

"Whew!" Stephanie said when the band finally took their last bow. "That was intense!"

"Almost as good as basketball practice," Malcolm observed.

"You guys," Maria said. "You have such one-track minds."

"Actually, two-track," Scott corrected her. "Basketball *and* food."

"Yup," Billy agreed. "How about Valdi's for pizza?" He looked at Stephanie. "How about it?" he said. "Will you let me buy? I can have my brother pick us up from Valdi's and drive you home in say . . . an hour?"

"Okay," Stephanie agreed. She was having a good time and didn't have to be home until ten o'clock.

They started out of the school. Dana reached into her pack and handed Stephanie three packages, wrapped in shiny blue paper. "One for Darcy, one for Allie, and one for you," Dana said. "You can open yours now, as long as you don't tell Allie and Darcy what it is."

Stephanie opened the package and unfolded a white T-shirt with a picture of a raccoon on it. It was Bingo, the little raccoon that Allie found and turned into the John Muir mascot for a while. "Friend of Wildlife," the shirt read.

"We made up the T-shirts to raise money for the wildlife shelter," Dana explained. "I figured that since the three of you cared about him so much— you ought to have T-shirts."

"I love it!" Stephanie said. "And so will Darcy and Allie!"

Fifteen minutes later Stephanie and her friends were walking toward the pizza parlor.

Just as Stephanie was going through the door, a tall, older boy made his way out of the crowded restaurant. He carried a box with a take-out pizza. He looked so familiar that Stephanie froze.

He looked almost exactly like Keir, except taller. He had the same blue eyes and black hair. The same tan skin.

Then Stephanie's eyes went to the boy behind him, and she felt her heart drop to the pit of her stomach. It *was* Keir. The older boy had to be his brother.

"Hi," Keir said stiffly.

"Hi," Stephanie replied equally stiffly.

Stephanie felt a tug on her hand. It was Billy. "Come on, Steph," he said. "We've got a booth."

Keir stared at her. Then he followed his brother out of the restaurant.

Stephanie took a seat beside Billy. She felt awful. *How did this happen?* she asked herself. The night started out so well. She was having such a good time.

How did everything go so totally wrong?

On Monday morning Stephanie got to school early. She was surprised to find Keir waiting at her locker. For a second her heart sped up hopefully. Then she realized that Keir had the same cold expression he'd had in Valdi's.

"I want to talk to you," Keir said bluntly.

"Sure." Stephanie took a deep breath. "What about?"

"About Friday night," he answered. "You told me you weren't going out with anyone. Then I see you in Valdi's with a guy who's holding your hand."

"Billy's just a friend," Stephanie explained.

"Oh, right. He looked like *just a friend.*"

Stephanie reached for her combination lock and tried to collect her thoughts. She reminded herself that she had just met Keir. She certainly didn't owe him any explanations.

So why did it matter so much if he believed her?

"Listen," she said. "I have a bunch of friends at Kennedy. Billy Dean happens to be one of them.

He invited me to their dance, mostly because it's been a while since I hung out with all of them."

"Then why did you give me that story about your vow and Friends First?"

"It *wasn't* a story," Stephanie told him. "That's all true."

"Then why weren't you with your best friends on Friday?"

"Because Billy invited me to that dance the week before. We'd already made plans."

Keir's blue eyes narrowed. "You expect me to believe that?"

"Believe what you want!" Stephanie snapped.

Keir folded his arms across his chest. "I get it," he said. "You've got this unbreakable vow with your friends that you only break when it's convenient."

"Not that it's any of your business, but I did *not* break my vow!" Stephanie shot back. She slammed her locker door closed. She was so angry that she barely noticed that the halls were filling up with students.

"Really?" Keir's voice was sarcastic. "So you told Allie and Darcy that you were going out with this Billy guy?"

Stephanie's eyes widened as she noticed Allie and Darcy standing just a few feet away.

"Not exactly," Allie answered. "Steph, what's going on?"

Stephanie groaned and shut her eyes. She wished she'd never gotten out of bed that morning. "Nothing!" she answered. "Absolutely nothing is going on."

"Then who's 'this Billy guy'?" Darcy asked.

"Billy Dean from Kennedy," Stephanie said miserably. "A week ago, when I went skating with him, he asked me to the Kennedy dance. And I went—partly because Dana said she had presents for you two."

Stephanie opened her locker again and took out the gift-wrapped packages. "Here," she said, handing them to Darcy and Allie.

"Wait a minute," Darcy said. "I talked to you Thursday night, and you didn't say anything about going to a Kennedy dance or dating Billy Dean."

"I am not dating Billy Dean!" Stephanie shouted.

The sudden silence in the hall told her that half the school had heard her.

"And I'm getting tired of having to explain myself," she went on in a whisper.

"We don't need explanations," Darcy snapped as the first bell rang.

"Right," Allie agreed. She narrowed her eyes. "We just don't like being lied to."

"Exactly!" Keir said.

All three went off to their first-period classes. Stephanie stood alone at her locker. *What is going on with my life?* she asked herself. *All I tried to do was be a good friend to everyone.*

And now I have no friends left!

CHAPTER
10

◆ ◀ ✦ ◆

On Tuesday morning Stephanie walked to school. She was glad for the exercise. She'd been blue ever since that awful fight the morning before. She still couldn't believe that not only were Darcy and Allie angry with her, but so was the boy she really liked.

Despite their argument, she couldn't help thinking that there was something really nice about Keir. And if she hadn't locked herself in with this crazy Friends First vow, she might find out what it was.

I just have to make things better, Stephanie resolved. *First I have to work things out with Allie and Darcy. And then I have to see if I can sort things out with Keir.*

Stephanie crossed the street and saw Kendra Davis coming out of the local corner store. She was carrying a large canvas tote bag filled with groceries.

"Hi, Stephanie," Kendra said. "I was hoping I'd run into you."

"You were?" Stephanie asked. Actually, she was glad to see Kendra. It was great to talk to someone who *wasn't* mad at her.

Kendra shifted the bag of groceries to her hip. "I just found out that I have to leave for L.A. on Saturday," she said. "For an audition for a sitcom!"

"That's fantastic!" Stephanie said.

"It will be if I get the part," Kendra agreed. "But the thing is, I won't be back in San Francisco until Monday night. And I was wondering if you could stop by my house on Sunday and feed my parrot. I could leave that video of my commercials for you to watch."

"Sure. I didn't know you had a parrot," Stephanie said. "What's he like?"

Kendra smiled. "Howie's a sweetie. Really smart and affectionate. But I should warn you— he has kind of a strange vocabulary."

"What do you mean?" Stephanie asked.

"I inherited Howie from a director friend who used to bring him to film sets," Kendra explained.

"Plus lately Howie's been listening to me rehearse. So he's picked up some weird phrases."

"A show-business parrot," Stephanie said. "I can't wait."

Kendra laughed. "Tell you what—I'll drop a set of keys by your house before I leave for L.A."

"Great," Stephanie said. "And good luck on the audition!"

Stephanie continued on her way to school. She felt a little more cheerful. After all, since no one else was speaking to her, she might as well hang out with a talking bird.

That afternoon Stephanie waited restlessly for the last bell of the day to ring. She glanced at the clock. It read 2:47. Three minutes to go. Stephanie couldn't figure out how, but she was convinced that Mr. Simmons's class mysteriously lasted longer than any other.

The bell finally rang. Stephanie was on her feet at once.

"Not so fast, Miss Tanner," the teacher said. "You don't want to miss your homework assignment, do you?"

Stephanie sat down again and waited impatiently while Mr. Simmons put a reading assignment on the board. Then she hurried out of the classroom, her mind on the *Scribe* meeting that was about to start.

Even though her personal life was falling apart, she managed to make progress on her column. As she walked toward her locker, Stephanie mentally reviewed the topic she'd chosen. She was going to write about the little things that every student could do to help the environment: recycling, walking or taking public transportation, using biodegradable soaps. . . .

Stephanie was surprised to find that Keir was waiting for her at her locker. She didn't know whether to be pleased—or alarmed.

"Hi," he said.

"Hi," she replied warily.

"Could we talk?" he asked.

"I-I've got a *Scribe* meeting to go to now," she told him.

"Then let me walk you over there," Keir offered. "I mean, I can't talk long, because I've got a guitar lesson, but there's something I need to clear up with you."

Stephanie was not in the mood for another argument. "If it's going to be anything like our last conversation—"

Keir's face flushed beneath his tan. "It's not, I

promise. I'd really appreciate it if you'd just hear me out."

Stephanie nodded. "Okay, I'm listening."

"I had no right to call you a liar," Keir began. "Or to tell you that your vow was dumb. I was totally out of line."

"Uh, thanks," Stephanie said. "For the apology, I mean."

Keir ran a hand through his black hair. "You know, I keep asking myself—how could I have two major arguments with a girl I barely even know? Well, I came up with an answer," he went on. "I realized that the reason I got so mad at you—both times—was because I like you. I mean, I thought you and I could really get along. And it made me angry to realize I wasn't even going to have a chance."

"But—" Stephanie started to say.

"Please. Let me finish," Keir said. "This is sort of hard to say," he added quietly. "When I realized you didn't want to go out with me, I just . . . lost it."

"I never said I didn't want to go out with you!" Stephanie protested.

"At any rate," he told her. "I thought maybe we could start all over again and be friends."

"Of course we can," Stephanie said. "But—"

"Good." Keir smiled with relief. "Because I'm the new kid in school and I'm just starting to meet people. I don't want you to think I'm a jerk."

Oh, man! Stephanie thought. *Has he ever got it wrong! I'm not even sure where to start.*

She shut her locker and began walking with Keir beside her.

"First of all, I do like you," she assured him. "I want to be friends, too."

Keir's eyes lit up with relief. "Then prove it to me," he said.

"How?"

"I need to show you—and me—that I'm totally okay with you dating this Billy guy. That I'm over it. So I think we should go on a double date this Friday. You and Billy, and me and Marina. We can play miniature golf at the new course that just opened."

Stephanie stared at him in disbelief. "Let me get this straight. You want me to go out with Billy while you date Marina? On the same date, that is?"

Keir smiled at her. "Sure. What do you think?"

Stephanie thought it was the worst idea she'd ever heard. But Keir was trying so hard to be friendly that she couldn't quite tell him that.

"Um, I-I—"

Keir looked at her expectantly.

"I don't really double-date," she finally said.

"This is just for one night," Keir assured her.

Stephanie thought quickly. She could try to get out of it—but that was exactly how she'd gotten Keir mad at her in the first place. She could tell him she liked him and wanted to go out with him, too. But that would be pretty embarrassing now that he wanted to go out with Marina.

Or, she realized, she could just grit her teeth, go on the double date, and get it over with. "Okay," she said at last. "I'll ask Billy."

"Great," Keir said. "Let's check in later this week."

"Great," Stephanie replied in a flat tone. She watched Keir jog off down the hall, her mind in a daze.

Well, at least Keir is talking to me now, she consoled herself. *Then again, I still seem to be dating "this Billy guy."*

Stephanie shook her head as she entered the Media Arts Room. Her life was going out of control.

And she didn't have a clue what to do about it!

CHAPTER
11

♦ ◄ ◆ ♦

"Knock, knock!" D.J. called, and opened the door of Stephanie's room.

Stephanie glanced up from her computer screen. "Come on in, Deej."

D.J. sat down on Stephanie's bed. "How come you've been holed up in your room all night?" D.J. asked. "I thought you were going to watch that mystery video with me and Michelle."

"Can't," Stephanie replied. "I've got to work on my new column for the *Scribe*."

"Again?" D.J. stretched out on the bed. "Sounds to me like that's the only thing you've been working on."

"That's because I can't get the *Scribe* staff to approve any of my topics," Stephanie explained. She turned away from her screen with a sigh. "I thought I had the perfect idea—that environmental one I told you about."

"And?"

"And it turns out that Quentin Baglio's computer column—which he already wrote—is about a kid's web site that deals with the exact same thing. Only the web site has super-cool graphics and Roger the Recycling Rodent."

D.J. bit back a smile. "It's tough to compete with Roger the Recycling Rodent."

"Tell me about it!" Stephanie moaned. "Yesterday's *Scribe* meeting was a disaster."

D.J. sat up. "So what are you working on now?"

"More topics," Stephanie said. "For example: 'John Muir Needs Art in the School to Encourage Future Artists.' You know, paintings on the walls, sculpture on the lawn. Creative stuff."

D.J. smiled.

"You hate it?" Stephanie guessed.

"No, I think it's good," her sister said. "But John Muir's not an art school. What about all those future doctors and mechanics and bankers and hairstylists and cooks?"

"I guess that's true," Stephanie admitted. She hit the delete button and scrolled down to her next topic. "How about: 'Volunteering for Charity Can Be Rewarding'?"

"Isn't that kind of obvious?" her sister asked.

Stephanie hit the delete button again. " 'Cliques Are Limiting and Dumb'?"

"That's not going to get rid of cliques," D.J. told her.

Stephanie put her head in her hands. "Well, I can't think of anything else!" she said. "I have to tell Ms. Blith to assign this column to someone else. Fast!"

D.J. stood up. "I'm sure you'll think of something," she said. "What are *you* most interested in?"

"The column isn't about me," Stephanie reminded her. "It has to be relevant to the whole school!"

"Maybe if you started off on a more personal tack, it would be," her sister suggested.

Stephanie picked up her head. "Like what?"

"Oh, I don't know." D.J. studied the ceiling. "How about . . . 'How Wonderful It Is to Have a Brilliant Older Sister'!"

Stephanie threw a pillow at her. "Out!" she ordered. "You are not helping!"

Seconds later the phone in the hallway rang and D.J. was back. "It's for you," she told Stephanie. Her voice dropped to a whisper. "It's a *boy!*"

"Maybe I should write about how totally

annoying older sisters are," Stephanie muttered. She walked out to the hallway and picked up the phone. "Hello?"

"Stephanie? It's Keir."

"Keir!" she said. "Oh, hi." She couldn't help it. Her heart was beating faster.

"I'm just calling to see if Billy is okay with our plans for Friday night," he said.

"Billy?" Stephanie echoed. Her heart slowed to its regular pace.

"Yeah. You were going to ask him about minia-ture golf."

"Right. Um . . . the truth is, I haven't asked him yet. I've been really busy. I'm still working on this column for the *Scribe*."

Keir was quiet for a moment, then said, "Well, I asked Marina. And she said it's fine with her."

"Terrific," Stephanie said weakly. "Then I guess I should call Billy."

"Okay, ask him if seven is a good time. Let me know what he says. Good night, Steph." Keir hung up.

Stephanie stared at the telephone receiver in dismay. Then she sighed and dialed Billy's num-ber.

"Hi," she said when Billy answered the phone. "I have a favor to ask."

"Name it," Billy told her. "I really owe you for helping me with Carrie."

"I need you to go on a double date with me," Stephanie explained. "This Friday night at the new miniature golf course."

"The one that looks like Jurassic Park?"

"That's it."

"Cool!" Billy agreed. "I've been wanting to try that place."

"Can you meet us there at seven?" she asked.

"Sure, but Steph—"

"What?"

Billy hesitated, then said, "You sound like you're inviting me to a funeral. What's wrong?"

Stephanie sat down on the floor and leaned back against the wall. "I-I'm just a little down tonight," she said.

"Just a *little?*" Billy echoed. "Come on, Steph. We're friends. What's going on? Why don't you want to go on this date?"

"It's a long story," Stephanie warned.

"I'm listening," Billy said.

Bit by bit Stephanie told Billy the whole story.

"Ouch," Billy said when she finished. "That sounds like a drag. You don't want to watch Keir going out with Marina if you really like him."

"I don't have a choice," Stephanie confessed. "If

I refuse, then Keir will think I'm feeding him another excuse. And I can't tell him I like him when he's interested in Marina."

Billy was silent for a moment, then said, "Look, if you really think you have to do it, we can at least make it fast."

"What do you mean?" Stephanie asked.

"On Friday night I'll . . . I'll fake being sick. I promise you it will be the shortest double date in history!"

Stephanie smiled. "You would do that for me?"

"In a heartbeat," Billy answered.

"You're a good friend, Billy," she said.

"So are you," he told her. " 'Night, Steph."

At least one person thinks I'm a good friend, Stephanie thought as she hung up. *Maybe things aren't quite as hopeless as they seem.*

Stephanie got to her feet and frowned. Michelle was sitting on the top stair of the staircase.

"You little sneak!" Stephanie said. "You listened to every word!"

Michelle shrugged. "It was more interesting than that movie. It had a seriously bad plot. It was obvious from the beginning that the manicurist did it."

Stephanie laughed. "So now my life is being compared to a bad movie."

"What I really want to know," Michelle said, trailing after her, "is why you keep agreeing to go on dates that you really don't want to go on."

Stephanie turned back toward her sister with a rueful smile. "That's a good question," she admitted. She sat down in front of her computer screen, her mind still on Keir and Billy.

"In fact," she murmured to herself, "it's an excellent question. Why *do* I keep agreeing to dates I don't want to go on? And what on earth am I going to do about it?"

CHAPTER
12

◆ ◀ ✦ ◆

Stephanie was the last one to arrive at the miniature golf course on Friday evening. Keir, Billy, and
Marina stood waiting by the entrance. Marina
wore a garnet-red sweater over faded jeans. Her
long dark hair lay loose over her shoulders.

She looks perfect, Stephanie thought. *Casual, nat-
ural, and pretty.*

Stephanie swallowed hard. She knew it was
going to be tough to watch Keir and Marina
together. At least Billy promised that the evening
wouldn't last long. So she'd better find a way to
act friendly while it lasted.

"Hi, everyone!" Stephanie said as cheerfully as
she could. "I see you've all introduced your-
selves."

"Well, Billy and I sort of met at Valdi's," Keir said.

"And Marina and I have been talking basketball," Billy filled her in. "Did you know that Marina played guard for her team in Wyoming?"

Marina rolled her eyes. "Fascinating, isn't it?" she joked.

"I think so," Keir said, gazing at Marina.

Stephanie looked away. *This is going to be harder than I thought*, she realized.

They all paid the entrance fee and walked through the gate made of fake rocks. The gate opened into a "cave" where they got golf clubs, balls, scorecards, and pencils.

Keir was the first one to step outside. He gazed around at the huge dinosaurs that filled the course. "Check it out," he said in amazement. "This place is surreal."

Stephanie stared up at a huge blue Tyrannosaurus rex. "Do you think dinosaurs were really blue?" she wondered aloud.

Keir shrugged. "Why not? They could have been pink or blue or polka-dotted for all we know."

Keir and Marina teed off first. Then Billy, then Stephanie. Both Billy and Marina got holes in one. Keir took two strokes, and Stephanie needed four.

By the time they finished the fifth hole, which was hidden in a mound between two nesting

96

pterodactyls, Stephanie felt like the odd one out. She took a look at the scorecard. It was even worse than she guessed.

"I have nearly five times as many strokes as you guys!" she moaned. "Are you all secret golf pros, or something?"

"Yes," Billy said seriously. "I spend every spare minute practicing miniature golf."

"Me too," Marina said. "I leave on tour next week."

"The Velociraptor Classic?" Billy asked.

"How did you know?" Marina replied.

"Well, they invited me, too," Billy explained. "Only I refused to wear those hokey madras-plaid pants."

Marina giggled. Keir raised his eyebrows at Stephanie. "They've lost their minds," he said.

"Golf brain," Stephanie diagnosed. "It seriously affects your ability to have an intelligent conversation."

Billy shot another hole in one, this time straight through the legs of an apatosaurus.

"You're just jealous," he said. "We basketball jocks have excellent coordination. Besides, dinosaurs like me."

Marina giggled again. "Maybe they have golf brain, too."

Marina is paying more attention to Billy than she is to Keir, Stephanie realized, a little surprised. Maybe it was because they were both tall, athletic, and crazy about basketball.

The question is, Stephanie thought, *is Billy interested in Marina?* It was hard to tell. Billy was so naturally outgoing and friendly, he talked to anyone.

They all moved on to the next hole, but had to wait. The couple in front of them was playing very slowly.

Stephanie sighed and glanced at Billy. He and Marina were laughing about something. *When, exactly, was he planning on getting sick?* she wondered.

Keir studied Marina and Billy and frowned. "Marina," he said, "do you want a soda or something from the snack bar?"

Marina appeared startled, as if she'd forgotten Keir was there. "Sure," she said. "I'll go with you. Do you two want anything?" she asked Stephanie and Billy.

"Nothing for me, thanks," Stephanie said.

"Nope, I ate dinner about twenty minutes ago," Billy added.

Stephanie waited until Keir and Marina were out of earshot. Then she turned to Billy and said, "Did you forget our plan?"

Billy blinked. "No. I just thought it would look suspicious if I got sick two minutes after we started playing. I figured after the ninth hole, I'd suddenly start feeling really bad."

Stephanie glanced at the couple ahead of them. They were on the eighth hole. The boy was giving the girl pointers on her swing. How could anyone take miniature golf so seriously?

"Getting to the ninth hole could take a while," Stephanie said.

"No more than twenty minutes," Billy promised. "Come on, Steph, aren't you having a good time? This is fun!"

"Fun? Sure," Stephanie muttered. She wanted to ask how Billy felt about Marina—but she saw Marina and Keir returning from the snack bar.

Keir carried a box of popcorn. "Want some?" he asked, holding it out to them.

"No, thanks," Billy said. He groaned and put his hand on his stomach. "I think the meatloaf I had for dinner is disagreeing with me. I don't feel so hot."

"Try some soda." Marina offered him her soft drink.

"That's okay," Billy said, grimacing. "I'm sure I'll feel better in a few minutes."

But Billy got sicker and sicker. Or that's what

Stephanie would have believed, if she hadn't known he was faking. He was an impressive actor.

"I think I'd better call it a night," Billy said after they finished the ninth hole. He was practically doubled over, as if he were in pain.

"I'll go with you," Stephanie offered. "To make sure you get home okay."

"You don't have to do that," Keir said. "My brother Jason owes me some transport. I did his chores for him last week. I'll go call him." Keir went over to a nearby phone.

Stephanie and Billy exchanged a panicked look. This was *not* the plan.

Keir was back a moment later. "Jason will be here in ten minutes," he told Billy. "You just have to wait at the gate."

"I'll walk you over there and wait with you," Stephanie volunteered quickly.

"We'll all wait with you," Marina offered.

Stephanie could not believe the way things were turning out. Two weeks ago she couldn't find a working phone. Tonight she could have used a bit of that phone jinx.

And it was suddenly clear that *she* was the one who should be playing sick. In ten minutes Billy would be on his way home, and she would be stuck on the golf course. For the rest of the evening it was going to be her and Keir and Marina—exactly what she didn't want!

Stephanie slept in the next morning. She was glad it was Saturday and that Michelle was already up and out.

How did my life get to be such a mess? she asked herself, but no easy answer came. So she pulled the covers over her head and scrunched her eyes shut.

Minutes later she opened them as she heard a knock on her door. *It isn't one of my sisters*, she decided. *They would have just barged in by now.* "Who is it?" she called.

"This is Danny Tanner, of *Wake Up, San Francisco*," her father said in his TV voice. "And I'm wondering why my second daughter is still in her room. Are you okay, Steph?"

"I'm fine, Dad," she answered.

Her father was silent for a moment, then said, "You don't sound fine. I think we should talk."

Stephanie mulled it over. If she said she wanted some privacy, her father would give it to her. But sooner or later, he'd want to talk. She might as well get it over with now.

She got up, put on her bathrobe, and opened the door.

Danny's eyebrows rose. "It's after ten. You've really been in bed all this time?"

Stephanie nodded.

"That's not like you, sweetie. Are you sick?"

"No."

Danny sat down in her desk chair. "Then what's wrong?"

"Not much," she answered. "Just that my entire life is a complete wreck."

"Are you having trouble in your classes?"

Stephanie dropped down on her bed. "Not really. Though my new biology teacher is a pill."

Her father smiled. "Well, if you're not having trouble in your classes, then your life isn't a *complete* wreck."

"It is," Stephanie told him. "Keir—this boy I like—thinks I don't like him. He also thinks I'm dating Billy Dean. Who should be dating Marina Rees, except now Keir has asked her out because he thinks I turned him down. Though I couldn't date anyone if I wanted to, because I promised Darcy and Allie I wouldn't. But Darcy and Allie think I broke my promise, so they're mad at me."

Danny gave a low whistle. "This isn't *Wake Up, San Francisco*. It's a soap opera!"

Stephanie smiled in spite of herself. "And I

haven't even told you about the trouble I'm having with my *Scribe* column."

Her father rubbed his chin. "Let's hold off on that for now," he said. "I know you just gave me a fast-forward version of the rest, but unless I'm mistaken, it sounds like a lot of misunderstandings."

"I guess that sums it up," Stephanie agreed in a glum tone.

"Misunderstandings aren't so terrible," her father pointed out. "It's not as though you tried to hurt anyone—"

"I was trying *not* to hurt anyone!" Stephanie exclaimed.

"And in the process you tied yourself up in knots." Danny gently pushed a strand of hair out of her face. "If you could magically have everything turn out right, what would happen?"

Stephanie thought for a moment. "Well, first of all, I'd have Allie and Darcy understand that they're my best friends for life. Without any rules or promises. We'd just be friends, there for each other. The way it's always been."

"What else?" her father asked.

"Keir would know that I am *not* dating Billy Dean. And that I would like to get to know him better." Stephanie squinted as she tried to figure out the rest of the formula. "And Billy and Marina would realize that they're perfect for each other!"

"That last item might not be up to you," her father said with a smile. "But I don't see why you can't straighten things out with Keir and Allie and Darcy."

"You make it sound so simple," Stephanie sighed.

Danny stood up and dropped a kiss on her forehead. "Maybe it is," he told her.

He went back downstairs, leaving Stephanie sitting on her bed, thinking. *Maybe I can work this all out*, she told herself. *I don't know what to do about Keir, but I bet I can get Billy and Marina together. And maybe even make up with Allie and Darcy.*

Smiling, Stephanie went out into the hallway to use the phone. She had a plan. And the first thing she had to do was invite Billy to the swing dance that night.

Just call me Cupid, she thought.

CHAPTER
13

♦ ◀ ✦ ♦

Becky pulled up in front of John Muir, and Stephanie got out of the car. "Do you really think I look all right?" she asked her aunt. She was wearing a short, flared, plaid wool skirt with a navy cardigan, navy tights, and Becky's saddle shoes.

"You look great—like you're ready to swing!" Her aunt smiled at her. "You'll do fine! Really. Don't be so nervous. Just have fun and call us if you need a ride home, okay?"

"I will," Stephanie promised, and started toward the school.

She crossed her fingers on both hands. Becky thought she was nervous about swing dancing. The truth was, Stephanie was nervous about everything else. Billy said he'd come to the dance.

And she was pretty sure that Marina, Allie, Darcy, and everyone else in the swing class would show. So the question was, would her plan work?

Three minutes later Stephanie took a deep breath and stepped into the brightly lit gym. To her surprise the floor was already crowded. Colored balloons hovered near the ceiling. The brassy sound of a big band blared from the speakers.

Liz, the swing teacher, stood on a platform at the front of the gym. A handsome, dark-haired young man stood next to her. They wore matching outfits—the blue of Liz's skirt was the exact same shade as his shirt.

Both Liz and the young man were snapping their fingers to the beat. Stephanie started snapping her own fingers and began to step in time to the music. She scanned the room, looking for her friends. *Darcy and Allie are here somewhere*, she told herself.

Her eyes were drawn to two terrific dancers in the center of the floor. They danced close, then spun out. The girl spun behind the guy, put her hands on his shoulders, and he flipped her neatly over his head. She landed perfectly. Never missing the beat, they began a series of complicated turns.

It's Marina and Billy! Stephanie realized with

106

amazement. Her first mission was already accomplished—and she didn't have to do anything!

Now on to Mission Number Two. Where were Darcy and Allie?

She gazed around the crowded dance floor. Finally she saw Allie's petite figure at the other end of the gym. Her back was to Stephanie. She was facing the boy she was dancing with—Grady O'Connor. And they were dancing together very smoothly, as if they'd danced together before.

That's weird, Stephanie thought. *Allie never mentioned anything about Grady.*

Stephanie's eyes widened as she spotted Darcy. She was dancing with Trey Jones. They were having a great time, talking and laughing together, and they seemed to know each other well, too.

What is going on? Stephanie asked herself. She remembered the phone call at Allie's house that Allie wouldn't take. And she remembered Darcy hanging up on her because of the call that came in for "her mom." And finally she remembered how both Darcy and Allie suddenly became fine about her canceling on them last night.

I bet Darcy and Allie have been dating all this time, Stephanie thought. *I bet they've been cheating on Friends First, too.*

"They look good together, don't they?"

Stephanie turned to her right and got her fourth major surprise of the evening. Keir was standing beside her. She'd never expected him to show up at the dance.

"I mean, Marina and Billy," he said.

"They look great," she admitted. She still wondered about Darcy and Allie, but she forced herself to put that aside. "Do you swing dance, too?" she asked Keir.

"Not like *that*," he answered. "I had a feeling Marina would be here. That's why I came. I didn't expect Billy to show."

Stephanie felt a twinge of guilt. "Uh . . . I invited him," she confessed. "Sort of to make up for the way last night turned out. But I had no idea he could dance that well," she added quickly.

Keir stared at them a moment longer, then shook his head and smiled. "Might as well join them," he said. He held out his hand to Stephanie. "Want to dance?"

"I can't dance like that either," Stephanie warned him.

"We'll give it our best shot," Keir promised.

Stephanie took his hand. "Have you ever done this before?"

Keir grinned. "Never."

Stephanie placed his hands so that one rested lightly on her arm, and his other hand held hers. "Okay then," she said. "Repeat after me. Slow, slow, rock it. Slow, slow, rock it!"

Together they chanted and stepped, rocked and kicked. At least half the time, they missed the beat, but Stephanie was enjoying herself.

Keir nodded toward Darcy and Trey. "Is Trey in your swing class, too?" he asked.

"No," Stephanie answered.

"I think they're all aliens," Keir said. "Disguised as middle-school kids so the rest of us will feel like clods."

At that moment the song ended, and Liz took the microphone. "May I have your attention, please?" the swing teacher said. "We're really glad to see such a great turnout tonight. And we can see that there are all different levels of dancing here. So we want to try something that should be easy for the ones who've had experience and fun for those who haven't.

"Everyone find a partner, please!"

Stephanie saw Allie and Grady whispering together. Darcy and Trey were still holding hands.

Keir held his hands out to Stephanie. "Partners?"

"Sure," Stephanie said.

"Luis and I will demonstrate," Liz went on. "Watch us once and then try it with us. This is called the jig walk." She demonstrated a kicking step, then counted out a sequence of kicks, rock steps, and spot turns.

"Think we can handle it?" Keir asked.

"We're pros," Stephanie joked.

But when she and Keir tried the sequence, they couldn't manage to kick at the same time. And on the last kick, when they faced each other, Keir kicked Stephanie in the shin.

"Ouch!" Stephanie cried, hopping on one leg.

"I'm sorry!" Keir said. He looked really upset. "Are you all right? I'm *really* sorry."

Stephanie rubbed her shin and forced a smile. "It's okay," she told him. "Really."

"Marina and Billy are doing it perfectly," Keir muttered.

"Aliens," Stephanie reminded him.

"Definitely. Want to try again?" Keir held out his hands. Then he stepped with his right foot when he should have stepped left. "This is hopeless," he groaned.

"And turn!" Liz called. "Then turn again."

Stephanie turned and turned—and turned right into Darcy.

"Ow!" Darcy cried.

"Well, watch where you're going!" Stephanie snapped.

"I *was* watching! You turned into me!" Darcy snapped back. "Really, Steph, what's your problem?"

"Maybe it's just that I can see I'm not the only one who had trouble keeping our promise."

"What do you mean?" Darcy asked indignantly.

"Now let's try it with music," Liz called out over their argument. She turned on the CD player.

"We've got to talk in the hall!" Darcy said.

"No problem," Stephanie told her.

She and Darcy stormed out of the gym, stopping only to bring Allie along with them.

"What's this all about?" Allie asked.

Darcy folded her arms across her chest. "That's what I want to know."

Stephanie spelled it out, "You and Trey, and Allie and Grady."

"For your information," Darcy said, "before tonight Trey and I just talked on the phone a few times."

"Really?" Stephanie said. "I didn't realize you could learn to dance so well together over the phone." She whirled to face Allie. "And how long have you and Grady been together?"

"We are not to-together!" Allie sputtered.

"Grady's in my math class. We just started talking tonight. What about you and Keir?"

"I never expected Keir to show up tonight," Stephanie explained. "I thought he hated dancing."

For a long moment the three friends glared at one another.

Stephanie pulled her ponytail off her neck. She was hot from the dancing. "Okay, so maybe you haven't actually been dating these last few weeks," she admitted. "But you know, I had a plan tonight."

"What kind of plan?" Darcy asked.

"I wanted to get Billy and Marina together. Which seems to be working out just fine. But I was also hoping the three of us would have fun dancing—like we always do—and we could just go back to being best friends again."

"It's a nice plan," Allie admitted. "But it doesn't solve our problem. You didn't put Friends First."

"Maybe the real problem is that we're making rules that are impossible to keep," Stephanie suggested.

"It was only for a month," Darcy reminded her.

"I know," Stephanie said. "But the vow was . . . crazy. Friends should make your life more fun. They shouldn't make you feel locked up."

"I seem to remember we all agreed to this vow," Allie pointed out.

"And Steph, *I* seem to remember that Friends First was your idea!" Darcy added.

Stephanie rubbed her forehead. "Maybe my ideas aren't always so brilliant," she said. "Our whole Friends First program—it just makes me feel like I have to prove something to you guys."

"Maybe you do," Allie agreed. She and Darcy exchanged a look, and Stephanie realized that they'd already discussed this.

"What it comes down to," Darcy said, "is that instead of being at our first sleepover, you went skating with Billy. And instead of being at our second one, you were at the Kennedy dance."

"And we agreed to no new projects," Allie said. "And I ran into Sue Kramer at the mall today, and she told me you're writing a new column for the *Scribe*."

"Plus, you didn't even check with us to see if we were going to the dance tonight," Darcy added.

Stephanie felt her temper flaring. "I didn't have to!" she said. "We all agreed to go when Liz announced it!"

"But you did check in with Billy Dean," Darcy pointed out.

"So what? Billy didn't know about the dance

here. I told him because I thought he and Marina would get along."

"And that would let you get together with Keir. Whom you're not supposed to be dating," Darcy said loudly.

"No!" Stephanie realized she was shouting and lowered her voice. "I told you. I had no idea Keir would show up tonight."

Allie put her hands on her hips. For someone so small, she could look very fierce. "The point is, we're supposed to put each other first." Her voice rose. "And as far as we can see, we're running fifth behind Billy Dean, Keir, Marina, and the *Scribe*."

"This isn't about rules, Steph," Darcy barked. "It's about who matters to you. And clearly, we don't!"

Stephanie watched in shock as Allie and Darcy turned their backs on her and marched back into the gym.

"Fine," Stephanie muttered. "Be that way!"

Her head was spinning. *How did I get to be the bad guy?* she asked herself.

"Steph?" Keir came out of the gym. "What happened? Why'd you disappear on me?"

"It's a long story," Stephanie told him.

"Try me," Keir said.

Stephanie sighed. "Let's just say that an hour ago, Darcy and Allie were mad at me. But I really believed we'd all show up at the dance, and I could make it better."

"And now?" Keir asked.

"Now it's worse than ever," Stephanie told him. "Because now I'm just as angry as they are!"

CHAPTER
14

◆ ◂ ◂ ◆

On Sunday afternoon Stephanie sat cross-legged on her bed and stared out the window. She was wearing her warmest sweats and her thick red hiking socks, and she was still freezing. It was gray and rainy and miserable outside. The weather reflected her mood perfectly.

She glanced down at the open spiral-bound notebook beside her. The lined page was filled with more topics for her column, which she had to turn in on Monday.

Which meant she had to finish it today.

Relax, Stephanie told herself. *All you have to do is write one measly column and feed Kendra's parrot.*

But her stomach was churning. She still felt awful about what had happened at the dance the night before. How was she supposed to write a column when her life was such a mess?

A knock sounded at her door. Stephanie scrunched her eyes shut. "Dad?" she asked. She knew her father had noticed her moping around the day before. She had a feeling it was time for another one of his talks.

"Nope, it's Jesse," her uncle answered.

Relieved, Stephanie got up and opened the door. Her blue eyes widened. Jesse, who lived in jeans and T-shirts, was wearing a gray suit, an ivory shirt, and a tie.

"What are you all dressed up for?" Stephanie asked.

"Becky and I are going to a wedding in Marin," Jesse reminded her.

"Oh, right," Stephanie said. "Your friend from college."

"Yeah." Jesse looked down at the floor for a moment. "Steph, I hate to bother you. But I need to ask a favor."

"What is it?"

"Our baby-sitter just called to say she's got the flu and can't come over," Jesse explained. "Becky's been on the phone to every other baby-sitter in the city, but no one's available on such short notice. And—"

"And I'm the only one home," Stephanie finished for him.

Jesse nodded. "I'm really sorry, Steph. But this is a fancy wedding. We can't just bring the twins along. And they're too young to leave on their own."

"No problem," Stephanie said. "I didn't have any plans to go anywhere, anyway. I'll be happy to watch Nicky and Alex."

"You're the best, Steph!" Jesse told her.

Stephanie smiled. "I'm glad someone thinks so."

Twenty minutes later Stephanie and the twins stood at the living room window and watched Becky and Jesse dash through the rain to their car.

"Mommy and Daddy are wet," Nicky observed.

"Very wet," Stephanie agreed. She smiled at her little cousins. "But we're warm and toasty. What would you guys like to do?"

"Play trains!" Alex said.

"Read us a story!" Nicky cried.

"Okay, we'll play trains for a while, and then I'll read you a story," Stephanie promised.

She and the twins spent the next half hour laying out the train tracks and miniature buildings. Finally, Nicky set the four cars and their caboose on the tracks. Alex turned on the switch.

At that moment the phone rang. Stephanie ran to get it.

"Tanner household," she said. She kept an eye on the twins as she spoke.

"Steph, it's Billy. I just wanted to thank you for inviting me to the swing dance last night."

"You're welcome," Stephanie said. "But how come you didn't tell me you were Fred Astaire?"

"That's kind of my deep, dark secret," Billy said.

"That you can dance?"

"It's actually my parents who do most of the dancing," he explained. "They're into ballroom. But every summer since I was five our family has spent the month of July at dance camp."

"That sounds like fun," Stephanie said.

"It is," Billy admitted. "But it's not something that the guys on the basketball team would understand. My brothers and I have sworn one another to secrecy."

Stephanie laughed. "Your secret's safe with me."

"I'll tell you another secret," Billy said. He hesitated a moment. "I really like Marina."

"That's not exactly a surprise," Stephanie told him. "You guys looked like something out of a movie on Friday night."

"That was fun," Billy said. "We're going skating next week."

"Did Marina say anything about Keir?" Stephanie asked.

"She said she was going to talk to him," Billy answered.

Great! Stephanie thought to herself. *Now maybe Keir and I can get together after all.*

"Steph—?"

"What?"

"I've got to go. But I just wanted to tell you—I have this feeling that everything's going to work out okay."

Billy hung up, and Stephanie returned to the twins. Nicky said he was ready for his story.

"Okay," Stephanie said. "Pick out a book, and I'll read it to you."

She watched the boys race over to the living room bookshelf, which was filled with picture books. They began to argue about which book to read. Comet added to the noise by barking loudly. A second later the doorbell rang.

What a day! Stephanie thought as she opened the door. She felt her jaw drop open.

Keir was standing there. Stephanie's heart skipped a beat.

"Hi," he said. "Are you busy right now?"

Stephanie gave a wide grin. "Sure," she said. "I'm baby-sitting my little cousins. But you can come in."

"Thanks." Keir stepped inside and Nicky walked up to him. "Stephanie has to read us a story," he announced.

Keir regarded him thoughtfully. "How about if I build you guys a fort now, and Stephanie reads your story later?"

"Cool!" the twins chorused.

"You don't mind if I take apart your sofa?" Keir asked Stephanie. "And your chairs?"

"Be my guest," she said.

Keir removed the cushions from the living room furniture. While the twins watched wide-eyed, he built a fort, complete with gate, moat, and tower.

"Now," Keir turned to Stephanie when the twins were playing, "I want to straighten things out with you."

Stephanie gulped hard. "You're not mad at me about Billy and Marina?"

Keir shored up a wall of the fort with an extra pillow. "No," he said. "Marina's great, but *you're* the one I'm really interested in. And I hope you're really not going out with anyone else."

Stephanie felt a warm, happy glow spread through her. "Are you sure?"

"Positive. The only reason I asked out Marina was because I thought you were going out with Billy."

"I'm not going out with anyone," Stephanie told him.

"Good," Keir said quickly.

Stephanie beamed at him. *This is so cool*, she thought.

"Then there's just one thing I want to know," Keir said. A puzzled look came into his eyes. "What's the story with Billy Dean?"

Stephanie explained the whole, long story. "It's just that my life has been so crazy lately," she finished. "And I really would like to date you. But I don't know how I'm going to work things out with Darcy and Allie."

"You haven't talked to them since last night?"

Stephanie shook her head. "We were all so mad . . . I just don't get it," she said. "They're my best friends, and I really love them. But lately I feel like my life is just too complicated. And the Friends First vow just made things worse."

"You know," Keir said thoughtfully, "you guys have been friends for so long that one little fight shouldn't break you up. You should just trust the friendship."

"I guess you're right," Stephanie said.

"And the good news is," Keir went on, "that your promise will be over soon."

Stephanie brightened. "That's right. But I still

have to find a way to make up with Darcy and Allie. And once I straighten things out with them, I've still got the column for the *Scribe* and swing class, and my regular writing assignments. And parrot-sitting," she added.

Keir raised one dark eyebrow. "I'm not even going to ask about that," he said. "But I think the column problem may be a case of first-time freeze."

"Which is?"

"The first time you do anything, it's scary," Keir explained. "This is the first time you're writing that column. Once you've done the first one, the others will be easier."

"I sure hope you're right," Stephanie said.

Keir looked at his watch. "I hate to say this, but I've got to run."

Stephanie rolled her eyes. "Maybe my column ought to be about how we spend all our time running around."

"Yeah, but some running around is fun," Keir told her. He put on his damp jacket. "I'm going over to the ice rink to play hockey."

Stephanie stood at the window and watched Keir disappear into the rain. She felt better than she had for a while. Maybe everything would be okay after all.

"Stephanie!" Nicky was tugging on her sleeve. "What are we going to do now?"

Stephanie smiled at him. "We're going to put on our raincoats and go feed a parrot!"

Kendra's door creaked when Stephanie pushed it open. She reached for the light switch in the hallway.

"Okay, guys," she told the twins. "You can look around. But remember—*don't touch anything!*"

"We won't," Alex promised solemnly.

"Howie, we're here!" Nicky called. "We're here to give you dinner!"

The boys shot ahead of her into the living room. Stephanie had never been in Kendra's house before. It was a narrow, two-story Victorian. The walls were covered with faded wallpaper, the furniture with deep green velvet. The house smelled of rosemary. It had a friendly feel to it.

Stephanie found a note from Kendra on a side table.

Stephanie—If you want to watch some goofy commercials, the video is in the VCR. Just turn on the TV and press play. Howie is upstairs in his room. Please give him a cup of dry food (in the blue canister) and fresh water. And let him out of his cage for a bit. Otherwise, he gets bored. Thanks—Kendra

"Where's Howie?" Nicky wanted to know.

"Uh, I think he's upstairs in his room," Stephanie replied. "Let's go feed him."

The twins raced up the stairs. Stephanie was close behind them. She looked down the long hall. Sure enough, one of the rooms had a hand-printed sign on it that read: Howie.

Stephanie pushed open the door.

"Wow!" Nicky said.

Howie's cage took up one whole side of the room. Inside he had branches to climb, a swing, and a little pond.

"Howie's very handsome," the bird told them.

"Yes, you are," Stephanie agreed.

She found the blue canister on a shelf behind her and measured out a cup of dry food.

"Can we let him out?" Alex asked. "Please?"

"Just for a little while," Stephanie said. She opened the cage. The parrot flew out at once and landed on a lamp shade.

Thump! Stephanie, Howie, and the twins all jumped as they heard the sound of something slam inside the house.

"What's that?" Alex asked, a quiver in his voice.

Howie ruffled his wings. "I will not be a french fry," he announced. "Never!"

"This place is weird," Nicky said.

"It's not weird," Stephanie told them. "I'll just go check on the noise. You guys stay here and keep an eye on Howie."

She left Howie's room and walked down the hall. She peeked in the next door. This was obviously Kendra's bedroom. The bed was neatly made, and everything was in place.

Stephanie checked the next room. The walls were lined with books. A desk sat to the side of the window. And then Stephanie realized what caused the noise. The window was open. The wind had blown over a wooden hat rack.

Stephanie shut the window and picked up the hat rack. She turned as she heard another loud *thump!*

"Stephanie!" Alex screamed. "Help!"

CHAPTER
15

◆ ◀ ✦ ◆

Stephanie raced back down the hall. "Alex, Nicky, are you all right?" she called.

She saw the door to Howie's room shake. "We're locked in!" Nicky cried. "We can't get out!"

"Just calm down," Stephanie said. "I'll get you out."

"Don't you think it's time you did something about your bad breath?" Howie asked loudly.

She twisted the doorknob and pulled. Then she twisted it the other way and pushed. The door didn't budge.

"Is there a latch on your side of the door? Or some kind of lock?" Stephanie asked the twins.

"Nothing," Nicky reported.

"I'm thirsty!" Alex said. "I need a drink of water."

"I have to go to the bathroom," Nicky added. *"Now!"*

"In a minute," Stephanie promised. "As soon as I open this door!" She twisted the knob again. The door didn't move.

Alex began to cry. "I'm thirsty!" he wailed. "And we're stuck with a bird!"

"I will not be a french fry!" Howie told them. "Never!"

Nicky began to cry, too. "I don't like it here! I want to go home!"

"Too much noise!" Howie squawked. "Quiet on the set! Quiet!"

Stephanie stifled a giggle. The situation was sort of funny—but she knew the twins were really panicked.

Nicky stopped crying. "I know," he said in a brave voice. Stephanie heard his footsteps cross the room. "I'll open a window! Then maybe we can climb out!"

"No!" Stephanie shouted. She no longer felt like laughing. "Don't open any windows. Howie will fly out. And it's too high to climb down. Do you hear me? *No windows!*"

But the boys didn't answer. Stephanie knew she

had to get them out quickly. Before someone got hurt.

"Don't move!" she told them. "Just sit there and talk to Howie. I'll be right back."

She raced down the hall to Kendra's room and picked up the phone on the night table. Quickly she dialed her own number. "Come on, Dad," Stephanie murmured. "Please be home and pick up the phone. Or Joey. D.J. *Anyone!*"

But all she got was the answering machine.

Stephanie stared at the telephone receiver. Should she call 911? No, her father had told her that was for serious emergencies. This was just a door that was stuck and two hysterical five-year-olds.

Stephanie bit her lip, undecided. Then she dialed Allie's number.

Stephanie felt her stomach clench as she heard Allie say, "Hello?"

"Hi, it's Stephanie."

There was a pause. "Oh," Allie said.

Stephanie hesitated. She recognized that cold tone. It meant that Allie was still mad. *This was a dumb idea*, Stephanie realized. *Allie won't even talk to me, let alone help me.*

"Stephanie, get us out of here!" Nicky shouted.

"I'm trying, Nick," Stephanie called back.

"You want speed? You want reliability?" Howie asked.

"Both would help," Stephanie muttered.

"Then I'm the computer chip for you!" Howie sang loudly.

"What is going on?" Allie sounded annoyed.

Stephanie took a deep breath. She didn't want to, but she had to ask for help. Her little cousins were depending on her.

"Allie," she said. "I need your help. And Darcy's, too, if she's there."

Stephanie heard someone pick up on the extension. "I'm here," Darcy said. She sounded every bit as cold as Allie had.

"Well, I'm at Kendra's," Stephanie said.

"Who's Kendra?" Allie asked.

"My neighbor. She lives across the street in that lavender Victorian," Stephanie explained. "I'm feeding her parrot while she's away and I had to take the twins with me because I'm baby-sitting them, and they just got locked in the room with Howie."

"Who's Howie?" Darcy wanted to know.

"The parrot!" Stephanie almost shouted.

"This sounds very complicated," Allie muttered.

"It's not," Stephanie said. "But they're really

scared, and I'm afraid they're going to do something dangerous, like try to climb out the window if I don't get the door open. I tried calling my house, but no one's home. I need help!"

Allie and Darcy were silent for a long moment.

Stephanie shut her eyes. *I can't believe it*, she thought. *We've been friends for all these years, and now they're mad at me when I really need them.*

"We'll be right there," Darcy said softly.

"ASAP," Allie added. "Just try to keep the boys calm."

"Right. And guys—thanks!" Stephanie put down the phone. She actually felt calmer already. Allie and Darcy were on their way.

Stephanie returned to her place outside Howie's door. "It's okay!" she told the twins. "Help is on the way. And in the meantime, I'm going to tell you a story. So just sit on the other side of the door and listen. Okay?"

"Maybe." Alex sounded sullen.

"You call *that* acting?" Howie asked. "You're fired!"

Nicky giggled. "It's going to be a funny story."

"I guess so," Stephanie agreed.

Stephanie was nearly at the end of her story when she heard the doorbell ring. "Be right back, guys," she told the twins. "Stay put!"

She ran downstairs and opened the door. Allie and Darcy were on the step.

"Where are the twins?" Darcy asked.

"I'll show you," Stephanie said.

The three girls ran upstairs. Allie took a screwdriver from the pocket of her raincoat.

"What are you doing?" Stephanie asked.

"Something I saw in a movie," Allie answered. "I'm going to unscrew the hinges. Then we can just lift off the door."

"That's brilliant!" Stephanie said. "If it works."

Darcy gave her a hug. "It will," she promised.

Ten minutes later Allie, Darcy, and Stephanie opened the hinge side of the door. Nicky and Alex were sitting on the floor. Howie was sitting on Nicky's shoulder with his head tucked beneath Nicky's chin.

"Are you guys okay?" Stephanie asked.

Nicky stroked the parrot's green feathers. "He likes me," he said happily.

"I think we'd better get Howie back in his cage," Stephanie suggested.

Howie straightened up and gave Stephanie a fierce look. "Do you have halitosis?" he demanded. "Do you?"

Behind her Stephanie heard Darcy and Allie cracking up.

Stephanie grinned as she reached for the parrot. "Okay, okay," she told her friends. "Now maybe you two geniuses can figure out how to get the door back on."

At seven o'clock that evening Stephanie curled up happily on one end of her bed. Allie sat across from her. And Darcy was stretched out on Michelle's bed. The three of them had gotten special permission from their parents for a Sunday sleepover.

"I still can't believe you two came to the rescue," Stephanie said. "Especially after that awful argument last night."

"We're still your friends," Allie said.

"You couldn't have kept us away!" Darcy added. She smiled at Stephanie. "You know, I have a confession. I did practice dancing with Trey. He and I had one little sort-of date last week."

Stephanie tried not to smile. "A sort-of date?" she echoed.

"It didn't start out that way," Darcy told her.

"And Grady and I talked on the phone before the swing dance," Allie admitted. "Last night was kind of our first date. But I didn't want to tell you guys."

"Because of Friends First?" Stephanie asked.

Allie nodded. "I felt kind of guilty."

"I've been thinking about what Stephanie said last night," Darcy added. "Maybe Friends First turned into too many rules. Maybe we ought to forget the rules and concentrate on the friendship."

"That sounds good to me," Allie agreed. "But what can we do to make sure we stay friends, when we're all so busy?"

Stephanie remembered what Keir said. "Maybe we don't have to do anything at all," she said. "Maybe we can just trust our friendship. After all, even though you were both mad at me, you both came through when I really needed you."

"We always will," Allie told her.

Darcy smiled. "When I heard you were in trouble, it wasn't even a question. We *had* to be there for you."

"And I'll always be there for you, too," Stephanie promised. Her eyes lit up with inspiration. "Oh, I've got it! I mean, you gave it to me! I finally figured out what my column is going to be about!"

"What?" Darcy asked.

"It's obvious," Stephanie told them. "And it's something that's relevant to every kid in John Muir. I'm going to write about what I know best— how important friends are!"

"This is getting way too sentimental," Darcy said with a laugh. "I think we've got to get to the important part of this sleepover."

"The popcorn?" Allie asked. She opened a paper bag that she'd set on the floor. "I made my special cheddar cheese popcorn right before I came over here."

"Not the popcorn." Darcy got up and unzipped her pack. She lifted out a large manila envelope. "The photographs!" she said. She opened the envelope and dozens of photos spilled onto the bed. "Check them out, girls!" she said.

Stephanie and Allie both rushed over to the bed.

"Here's the pink bunny rabbit!" Stephanie cried with delight.

"Give me that!" Allie snatched it from her.

"And here's that brilliant haircut!" Darcy said. She held up a photograph of Stephanie. Her hair was cut at about fourteen different lengths.

"That haircut *was* kind of radical," Allie said admiringly. "I mean, I could have a career as a hairstylist one day."

"Spare us," Stephanie pleaded. She rummaged through the mound of photos and picked up one near the bottom. "This is it," she said. "This one says it all."

The picture showed three sixth-grade girls holding hands. They were dressed up for Halloween. Each wore leotards, tights, boots, and a satin sash across her chest. On their heads sat homemade gold-foil crowns. Stephanie's crown came down over her forehead.

Stephanie looked at her friends, a question in her eyes. Laughing, Darcy and Allie joined hands with her. They began to chant.

> *Girls together, girls having fun,*
> *Girls to the rescue—*
> *Girl Power, everyone!*

A brand-new series starring Stephanie AND Michelle!

FULL HOUSE™

SISTERS

When sisters get together...
expect the unexpected!

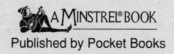
A MINSTREL® BOOK
Published by Pocket Books

2012-02

FULL HOUSE Stephanie™

PHONE CALL FROM A FLAMINGO	88004-7/$3.99
THE BOY-OH-BOY NEXT DOOR	88121-3/$3.99
TWIN TROUBLES	88290-2/$3.99
HIP HOP TILL YOU DROP	88291-0/$3.99
HERE COMES THE BRAND NEW ME	89858-2/$3.99
THE SECRET'S OUT	89859-0/$3.99
DADDY'S NOT-SO-LITTLE GIRL	89860-4/$3.99
P.S. FRIENDS FOREVER	89861-2/$3.99
GETTING EVEN WITH THE FLAMINGOES	52273-6/$3.99
THE DUDE OF MY DREAMS	52274-4/$3.99
BACK-TO-SCHOOL COOL	52275-2/$3.99
PICTURE ME FAMOUS	52276-0/$3.99
TWO-FOR-ONE CHRISTMAS FUN	53546-3/$3.99
THE BIG FIX-UP MIX-UP	53547-1/$3.99
TEN WAYS TO WRECK A DATE	53548-X/$3.99
WISH UPON A VCR	53549-8/$3.99
DOUBLES OR NOTHING	56841-8/$3.99
SUGAR AND SPICE ADVICE	56842-6/$3.99
NEVER TRUST A FLAMINGO	56843-4/$3.99
THE TRUTH ABOUT BOYS	00361-5/$3.99
CRAZY ABOUT THE FUTURE	00362-3/$3.99
MY SECRET ADMIRER	00363-1/$3.99
BLUE RIBBON CHRISTMAS	00830-7/$3.99
THE STORY ON OLDER BOYS	00831-5/$3.99
MY THREE WEEKS AS A SPY	00832-3/$3.99
NO BUSINESS LIKE SHOW BUSINESS	01725-X/$3.99
MAIL-ORDER BROTHER	01726-8/$3.99
TO CHEAT OR NOT TO CHEAT	01727-6/$3.99
WINNING IS EVERYTHING	02098-6/$3.99
HELLO BIRTHDAY, GOOD-BYE FRIEND	02160-5/$3.99
THE ART OF KEEPING SECRETS	02161-3/$3.99
WHAT CAN YOU GROW ON A FAMILY TREE	02162-1/$3.99